JOE and the Lightning Pony

VICTORIA EVELEIGH

Illustrated by Chris Eveleigh

Orion
Children's Books

First published in Great Britain in 2013
by Orion Children's Books
a division of the Orion Publishing Group Ltd
Orion House
5 Upper St Martin's Lane
London WC2H 9EA
An Hachette UK Company

1 3 5 7 9 10 8 6 4 2

The Orion Publishing Group's policy is to use papers that
are natural, renewable and recyclable products and made
from wood grown in sustainable forests. The logging and
manufacturing processes are expected to conform to the
environmental regulations of the country of origin.

A catalogue record for this book
is available from the British Library.

ISBN 978 1 4440 0592 9

Printed in Great Britain by
Clays Ltd, St Ives plc

www.orionbooks.co.uk

This book is dedicated to the talented few
who know what it's like to ride in the
Prince Philip Cup.
I have only ever watched in awe,
and wondered!

Chapter 1

J oe zipped up his jacket, checked there were gloves among the pony nuts and chaff in his pockets, took his riding hat off the shelf, opened the back door and hesitated.

Rusty bounded into the sleety rain with a joyous bark.

The countryside looked cold, grey and uninviting. It was difficult to remember how green Newbridge Farm had been when they'd moved in last summer – impossible to imagine the sun-baked fields now, in the muddy depths of winter.

I'm sure it never rained this much in Birmingham, Joe thought. Perhaps I just didn't notice, being indoors most of the time. He pulled the hood of his jacket up and made a dash for the old farmyard, wincing as ice-cold drops splashed against his face.

Three horses whinnied from their stables.

As Joe approached, Lady pawed at her door impatiently.

"Stop that, you hooligan." He paused to rub her broad forehead, and she bulldozed into his jacket with her hairy muzzle, seeking out the pony nuts in his pocket. She didn't look like a "Lady" at all, with her thick-set body and haphazard black-and-white markings. Her shaggy winter coat, which attracted mud like a magnet, did nothing to enhance her appearance either. Even so, she would always have a special place in his heart because it was she who'd got him riding again. And Lady didn't realise it, of course, but if Joe hadn't persuaded his parents to give her a second chance, she and Lightning could have had a very different future – or no future at all.

He moved on to Lightning. She bent her elegant neck to greet him, her nostrils flickering gently. He still couldn't really get his head round the fact that he had a pony, let alone this one. Everything about her was pretty well perfect, except for her feet. Perhaps even they were a good thing, though, because if she hadn't appeared to be incurably lame her previous owner wouldn't have given her away for free when Mum had bought Lady.

Lightning was the reason why Joe didn't mind getting up on a bleak Sunday morning in mid-December. Chris and Caroline had arranged to meet him so they could go for a ride together. Chris was the farrier who'd suggested trying to cure Lightning's lameness by taking her shoes off and giving her the right balance of food and exercise. Touch wood, it seemed to be working.

Caroline, Chris' stepsister, was in the same year as Joe at school. Could she be another reason why he didn't mind getting up early to go for a ride? If so, he definitely wouldn't admit it to anyone, least of all himself.

Lady banged at her stable door again.

"Okay, okay. Hang on a minute," Joe said, moving on to the next horse, always careful not to let any of them feel left out.

Ella's Tribute, a big bay thoroughbred, was the first official resident of The Hidden Horseshoe Sanctuary – Mum's new venture at Newbridge Farm. The idea was to provide a relaxing rehabilitation centre where horses with problems could be treated and go on to lead happy lives.

"Morning, ET. Sleep well?" Joe asked, knowing full

well what the answer would be if she could talk. As usual, she'd worn a path in the bedding around the edge of her stable where she'd walked round and round all night long. "You'll never get better and win races again if you don't rest your legs, you know," he said, stroking her rigid neck.

The owner of a high-maintenance horse like ET wasn't likely to keep her if she couldn't race or do anything useful. Horses cost a huge amount to look after, and most owners wanted something back in return. At least ET had been given the chance to come right. Joe couldn't bear to think of what might happen to her if she didn't. "You don't realise how important it is, do you?" he said, picking a piece of straw out of her forelock.

She nudged Joe, then her attention switched to some distant point. She stood with her head erect, whinnied, withdrew into her stable and paced around again.

Joe went into the tack room and mixed up three feeds: pony nuts, alfalfa mix and supplements for Lady and ET, and a couple of handfuls of pony nuts for Lightning. She'd get a good meal when they returned from their ride. One of the many things Chris had taught him was that horses shouldn't have a lot to eat just before they were ridden.

ET pinned her ears back and looked positively evil

as Joe approached with her breakfast. He'd found she backed off when he entered her stable, but he still didn't trust her completely. He edged past, tipped her feed into the manger, ducked underneath her neck and left as quickly as he could. She ate frantically, pawing at the air with alternate forefeet, as if miming a shovelling action.

I'd love to know what's made her such a bundle of nerves, Joe thought. He hurried on to give Lady her feed.

She thrust her head into the bucket as he walked into her stable, nearly knocking it out of his hand.

"Get over, you greedy pig," he muttered, pushing against her so he could squeeze between the wall and the solid bulk of her body. It's lucky horses are vegetarians, he thought. If Lady were a carnivore she'd be terrifying.

Lightning waited politely, and ate her nuts with unhurried enjoyment while Joe groomed her. Even though she wasn't clipped, she had such fine hair that Joe had bought her a turnout rug to wear in the field during the day and a stable rug to wear at night. The rugs kept her clean as well as warm, which was ideal because grooming horses caked in mud wasn't his idea of fun.

He'd nearly finished tacking up Lightning when there was a clatter of hooves in the yard. "Good timing!" he called. Glancing over the stable door, he noticed that Chris was riding Chocolate Buttons and Caroline was on another thoroughbred horse. "Where's Treacle?" he asked.

"I've got him here," Chris said. "We thought Emily might like to come too. I can lead her off Buttons."

Joe took a proper look and saw Treacle, Caroline's little Dartmoor pony, standing happily between the two thoroughbreds, his large, inquisitive eyes peering through his dripping forelock.

"I think Emily's having a lie-in," Joe said. She wouldn't want Chris and Caroline to know that, but it irritated him that she always told everyone how much she loved horses when she rarely helped look after them.

"Oh. Can you go and see?" Chris asked.

"Okay." Joe hitched Lightning's rein underneath her stirrup for safety, and trudged back to the house. He'd been getting on better with his younger sister since they'd moved to Newbridge Farm but, even so, he enjoyed spending time alone with the horses and riding with Caroline and Chris. He'd turned out to be the one who really liked horses and was keen enough to do the hard work as well as enjoy the fun. Horses had become *his* thing, and he wanted it to stay that way.

Chapter 2

E mily was very much awake, dressed, and over-
joyed at the prospect of a ride in the pouring rain.

Treacle jogged alongside Buttons while Emily
chatted happily to Chris and Caroline. Joe hung back
with Rusty and Chris' black Labrador, Bramble.

The rain turned into sleety snow, which lay white
for a moment before melting into slush. Chris said
they'd take the short route back to Lucketts Farm: up
the road on the opposite side of the valley, then along
the bridlepath that ran over some fields towards the
river again.

They picked their way carefully down the hill and over a narrow bridge. Lightning slipped once or twice, and Joe's heart lurched each time, but she cleverly managed to save herself.

Once over the bridge, the horses started dancing about, eager to have a sprint up the long hill.

"We'll just walk today," Chris said. He didn't say why, but Joe was sure it was because of Emily.

The two thoroughbreds jogged on the spot and snatched at their bits in frustration. Joe knew just how they felt.

Eventually they arrived at Lucketts Farm. Chris and Caroline stabled and fed their horses and Treacle, and then they all went into the indoor school with Lightning.

"Don't worry about taking off her saddle and bridle," Chris said. "I'll lunge her with you on top today. Give you a riding lesson at the same time."

If anyone thinks they can ride, a lunge lesson without stirrups will soon sort them out, Joe thought as he bounced around uncomfortably while Chris bombarded him with instructions: "Look up, keep your hands still, sit tall and relax your lower leg . . ."

A stitch niggled in Joe's side and spread underneath his rib cage. He didn't want to ask to stop, especially with Emily and Caroline watching, but if he carried on for much longer there was a distinct possibility he'd seize up completely and fall off.

"And wa-alk," Chris said in the calm sing-song voice he used when lunging. "Whoa-oa. Stand."

Oh, the relief!

"Great." Chris coiled up the lunge line in his hand. "Terrific."

Surely my riding wasn't that good, Joe thought.

Chris unclipped the line and gave Lightning a gentle pat. "As far as I can see, she's a hundred per cent sound. Congratulations, Joe. All your hard work looking after her and giving her regular exercise has paid off. You've got yourself a really nice pony there."

"Brilliant!" Caroline said. "Just in time for our Pony Club Christmas rally. It's going to be here on the Sunday before Christmas. You must come!"

"But I'm not a member," Joe replied.

"That doesn't matter. You're allowed a try-out session before you join. You'll *have* to become a member, anyway, now Lightning's fit and well."

"I don't know. I mean, it's a girl thing, isn't it?" Joe imagined his old friends in Birmingham rolling around laughing at the thought of him joining the *Pony Club*.

"Rubbish!" Caroline retorted. "Several boys are members – Simon Courtenay, for one."

Simon was in the year above at school. He was one of those self-confident types who always had a band of followers in tow.

"I'll think about it," Joe said.

"Great. Mum's organising it all, so I'll ask her to put your name down." Caroline turned to Emily. "You can come, too, if you want. Treacle will be free because I'm going to try out Simon's old pony, Minstrel."

Emily grinned. "Thanks!" she said. "Thanks a lot!"

"That's settled, then," said Caroline. "You're both booked in. It's not a serious rally, just fun and games. You'll love it!"

Chapter 3

The last week of term was a sort of rehearsal for Christmas, with unusually jolly teachers, decorations everywhere, appropriately themed lessons, a postbox for cards in the entrance hall, Christmas lunch and a carol concert. Going home to a house where preparations had barely begun was rather an anti-climax.

Still, as Emily reminded Joe over and over again, the Pony Club rally was on Sunday – two days after the end of term – so that would boost their Christmas spirit. Joe wished he could share her enthusiasm. He was beginning to wish he hadn't agreed to go. Everyone else will know each other and they'll be brilliant riders, he worried. I'm bound to do something wrong and make a fool of myself.

All his fears were confirmed as soon as he rode into Lucketts Farm on Sunday afternoon. The yard was full of girls wearing cream-coloured jodhpurs, short riding boots and green sweatshirts with Bellsham Vale printed around a bold Pony Club logo on them. Most of them had decorated their hats and their ponies with something festive, and they were cooing, giggling and exclaiming over tinsel browbands, Santa-style leg and tail bandages, glittery hoof oil and bright ribbons. In the centre of the crowd was Emily, who'd arrived beforehand to get Treacle ready. She'd obviously been lent some of Caroline's outgrown clothes, because she was wearing the right uniform. Her sweatshirt was rather faded, but that helped her to blend in. Treacle stood good-naturedly by her side, wearing felt reindeer antlers and a sparkly numnah.

Joe felt like the only person who hadn't made an effort at a fancy dress party, with his everyday dark brown jodhpurs, long boots and black sweatshirt, chosen in an attempt to look cool and inconspicuous. He'd heard that Pony Club instructors were very strict about clean ponies and tack, so he'd spent ages grooming Lightning and polishing her saddle and bridle. He needn't have bothered. For this rally, at least, the main requirement seemed to be as much horsey Christmas bling as possible.

Caroline spotted him and waved. Several people looked in his direction and then continued talking. He'd have to go over now. He nudged Lightning forward. She went willingly, with an extra spring in her step.

"Hi, Joe!" Caroline called. "Come and meet everyone."

"Everyone" turned out to be a few girls he knew from school – looking very different in their riding gear – and several others he'd never met before. Joe answered endless questions and asked some in return. Soon he was the centre of attention.

Perhaps the Pony Club isn't so bad after all, he thought, his head awash with the names of girls and ponies: Sarah and Flicka, Hattie and Purdie, Gemma and Copper . . . he'd never remember them all.

Sarah had dressed up as a glamorous fairy, and her pony was wearing a rug decorated like a Christmas tree, set off with green leg bandages and glittery hoof oil.

A horse transporter drove into the yard. With a sinking feeling, Joe read the sign on the back: *Courtenay and Farrell Solicitors: Working For You and the Countryside* followed by a web address and telephone number.

"Hey! Simon's arrived!" Sarah shouted.

The other girls watched as the gleaming silver transporter backed into a space at the end of the line.

It looked as if Simon had a pretty big fan club.

At last everyone mounted their ponies and went into the indoor school where Caroline's mum, Tracey, was waiting.

First they rode around the indoor school to warm up their ponies, and played a mounted version of *Simon Says* – accompanied by giggles from the Simon Courtenay fan club and smirks from Simon.

Joe felt silly taking part in a game he hadn't played since pre-school, surrounded by tinsel-clad girls on ponies. He was so busy thinking about how uncool it was that he followed a command not preceded by "Simon Says" and was the first person to be eliminated.

Emily came third and was given a large yellow rosette, which she tied to Treacle's bridle for all to see.

The next game was a mounted version of musical chairs, with old potato sacks instead of chairs. When the music stopped they had to dismount, lead their ponies and claim a sack by standing on it.

Joe's mood wasn't improved when Simon beat him

to the only spare sack, and he found himself watching from the sidelines again. Simon, Caroline and Sarah got on their ponies by vaulting, which looked really impressive. One moment they were standing on the ground, and the next they were in the saddle. Joe wanted to learn how to do that.

Several other games and a quiz followed, but he didn't do well in any of them. There was a break for tea and then Tracey called, "Listen up, everyone! Time for a few team races to finish off. I've split you into five teams: Snowballs, Reindeer, Elves, Mince Pies and Crackers."

Joe listened for his name, but he wasn't a Snowball, Reindeer, Elf or Mince Pie.

"And last, but not least, the Crackers!" Tracey announced. "Simon, Jess, Gemma, Sarah and Joe." She smiled. "Thought you two boys might appreciate some male solidarity."

Simon didn't look pleased.

Joe joined his team-mates. They were a mixed bunch. Jess was still on the leading rein, and was being led by her dad. Gemma was riding a large, hairy pony called Copper. Joe had already noticed how well Sarah rode her swift little golden dun pony, Flicka. And Simon . . . he was good, and he knew it.

The parent helpers rushed around, putting poles in neat rows.

"Okay," Tracey said. "You all know the rules of bending, don't you?" She ran up the arena. "Weave in and out of the poles – like so – turn around the top pole, and weave back again. Pass your baton to the next person in your team *only* after you've crossed the line. If you miss a pole you have to go back and if you knock it over you have to pick it up again. Is that clear?"

"Yes," everyone chorused.

Tracy searched around in the heap of equipment at the end of the school. "We haven't got enough batons, so you'll have to touch hands instead. Remember to be behind the start line, though. And I seem to have lost my flag for starting races, so I'll say 'Ready, steady, go' instead. Okay?"

Several people nodded or mumbled "Okay" in reply.

Simon wasted no time in becoming self-appointed leader of the Crackers. He gathered his team around him. "Right, you go first, Joe. That way, if you mess it up we'll be able to sort it out. Then it'll be Gemma, Jess and Sarah. I'm the fastest, so I'll go last."

Joe could feel Lightning tensing underneath him as he stood on the starting line. Why did he feel so anxious? It was only a silly game, after all. He fixed his eyes on the nearest pole.

"Ready, steady, *go!*" Tracey shouted.

At the word *go*, Lightning leapt forward like a racehorse let out of a starting stall. It was all Joe could do to hang on as she galloped in and out of the poles. Had he missed any or knocked them over? He wasn't too sure. All he knew was they should be slowing down because the end pole was coming up and they'd have to go round it. He sat up straight and felt the reins. She responded instantly, bunching up and taking him around the last pole at such an angle that he was nearly thrown off sideways. Then they were off again, flat out towards the cheering mob at the end of the arena. He'd plough straight into them at this rate. His hand – he must hold out his hand! He felt his palm slapping against Gemma's, sensed ponies moving aside and saw the timbers of the wall getting closer. Lightning slid to a halt and spun to the right to avoid a head-on collision. Shock waves whipped through Joe, and he lost all sense of direction as he fell forwards and wrapped his arms around his pony's neck. With a body-wrenching effort, he managed to struggle back on top with as much dignity as he could muster, only to find that the saddle had slipped round. He'd have to get off anyway, to straighten it.

By the time he'd sorted himself out, all eyes were on Simon, who leapt into action when Sarah whizzed by, and set off at a flat-out gallop while the riders from all the other teams were still at the top of the arena. Joe tried not to be impressed as Simon weaved through the poles with millimetres to spare, took the turn at an angle which defied gravity and then dashed back again, way ahead of anybody else.

Three more team events followed: a ball and bucket race, mug race and flag race. Lightning seemed to know instinctively what to do, and to Joe's delight his team came second, third and first. Caroline had been right after all – this was really good fun.

Tracey added up the scores for each race, and read out the results from the bottom up.

". . . And so the winners, with seventeen points, are the Crackers!" Tracey announced.

There were whoops and cheers from everybody, including a crowd of parents who were watching in the viewing gallery. Looking up, Joe noticed Mum, Dad and their neighbour, Nellie, among them. He hoped they'd come late and had only seen the best bits.

"I thought you'd never done games before," Simon said, slightly accusingly, as they lined up for their rosettes.

"I haven't." Joe took the first rosette Tracey held out for him. "Thanks."

Tracey stroked Lightning. "I bet she has, though. She's well-named, isn't she?"

Chapter 4

Christmas in Birmingham had meant a day spent indoors with the family, giving and receiving presents, eating, watching TV and trying to avoid arguments with Emily.

At Newbridge Farm, though, it was as if Christmas had been reinvented. It started on Christmas Eve, when they all went to Coltridge, their nearest village, for a party in The Ewe and Lamb. Martin, whose parents ran the pub, was one of Joe's best friends.

Joe's family sat with Caroline's for the buffet supper. As they ate, Joe couldn't help overhearing

Mum talking in hushed tones to Tracey.

"Are you really sure about this?"

"Of course we are, Jackie. We wouldn't have offered otherwise."

"It's a huge responsibility."

"Don't worry. We know you'll look after—"

Martin tapped Joe on the shoulder. "Fancy a game of darts in a minute, while the board's free? Rob and Darren are up for it."

"Er, great," Joe said, still trying to eavesdrop on Mum's conversation. He picked up something about *a lovely surprise tomorrow* . . .

"You okay?" Martin asked.

Joe gave up trying to listen. "Yup, fine." He got up and joined his friends.

The darts game was followed by bar billiards, and then everyone crowded into the alley at the back of the pub for a skittles match which lasted until closing time.

As they came out of the pub the church bells were ringing for Midnight Mass and everything sparkled in the moonlight.

Mum gazed up at the starry sky. "Ah! This is how Christmas should be!"

"Magical, isn't it?" Dad said, giving her a hug.

*

Joe woke next morning with warm doggy breath on his face and a cold wet nose against his cheek.

"Gerraway, Rusty."

With a delighted "Wruf!" Rusty leapt onto the bed and started to lick Joe's face and arms enthusiastically.

"Gerroff! Ugh, no!" Joe tried in vain to pull the duvet over his head. No escape. "Okay, okay, you win." He wriggled out of bed and dressed as quickly as possible. His clothes felt as if they'd been in a freezer.

In Birmingham their house had been centrally heated, but here at Newbridge Farm there were no such luxuries – just an oil-fired range in the kitchen, a wood burner in the living room and some ineffective electric heaters in the bedrooms.

For a moment Joe wondered what the family who'd bought their house were doing. Had they put the tree where passers-by could see it in the sitting room? Would they open their presents in their pyjamas, blissfully unaware of how cold it was outside? He looked out of his bedroom window. Thick white frost glistened in the early morning sunshine. The ground would be too hard for riding. Probably just as well, with so much happening – church and lunch and everything. They didn't usually go to church on Christmas morning, but the pupils at Dad's school were singing carols during the service. Emily had been practising for weeks.

Joe heard Mum and Dad going downstairs, followed a moment later by Emily, who called out, "Wakey, wakey! It's Christmas!"

He felt a familiar tingle of anticipation. He remembered the conversation he'd overheard in the pub: "A lovely surprise tomorrow . . ."

Joe's presents were all shapes and sizes this year: a stick-like thing with a spiral of wrapping paper and tape around it, a knobbly parcel, a flattish squidgy package, a neat rectangular one, something in a bin liner with a piece of tinsel on top because it was too big to wrap, and a couple of envelopes. They turned out to be a fishing rod, a fly-tying kit, some cream-coloured jodhpurs, a book by an American horseman he'd seen on TV, a luxurious-looking dog bed for Rusty to have in the bedroom, a rod licence and some cash which Mum said was a bonus for all the work he'd done with the horses.

Apart from the money, all those gifts would have seemed bizarre a year ago, but so much had changed. Martin had introduced him to the delights of fly-fishing, he'd become interested in horses again, almost by accident, and he'd acquired Rusty – or Rusty had acquired him. His transformation into a country boy had been remarkably quick. Perhaps he'd always been one, deep down.

Emily's presents also reflected the changes in her

life, but not in her favourite colour. She squeaked with delight as she unwrapped pink wellies with red hearts all over them, a pink winter coat, a book about ponies and pony care, a large toy stable for her model horse collection and a pink bag with a cartoon pony on it.

"Ooh! A grooming kit!" she exclaimed, naming each item as she pulled it out of the bag and placed it carefully on the sitting room carpet: "Dandy brush, body brush, curry comb, water brush, hoof pick, mane comb and sponge."

"You'll have to help me groom the horses now," Joe said.

Emily's eyes opened wide with indignation. "I already do! I often help!"

"Oh? Like when?"

Mum stood up. "Stop that, you two! Joe, come and do the horses with me. Emily, you can peel vegetables with Dad."

Joe did a double-take as he walked past the unused stable by the feed shed. It had been full of all sorts of things, from old hay racks and furniture to a lawn mower and chainsaw, but it had been cleaned out and bedded down with fresh straw. "When did that happen?" he asked.

With unconvincing astonishment Mum said, "Well

I never! Some elves must have done it. I expect Santa's reindeer needed a rest after all their hard work."

"Ha, ha, very funny. Are we getting another horse?"

"Maybe. You'll have to wait and see."

Joe grinned. "What's it like? What's it called?"

"My lips are sealed."

"Mu-um!"

"Help me feed these horses before Lady kicks her door down."

Joe tried again as he followed Mum out to the field, but he couldn't prise any more information out of her. Mum led Lady and Lightning while Joe hung onto ET, who skittered around on the rock-hard turf. She galloped off with her tail in the air as soon as Joe let her go. Lady and Lightning followed half-heartedly, but soon gave up.

"I hope the new horse isn't another nutty thoroughbred," Joe said, secretly thinking the exact opposite.

Mum inhaled sharply and put her hands over her eyes as ET took a corner too fast and nearly slid over. "No, it's not. My nerves wouldn't stand it."

"Oh."

Before Joe could ask any more questions, she said, "Not a word about the stable to Emily, okay? We'd better hurry up and have breakfast, or we'll be late for church."

Chapter 5

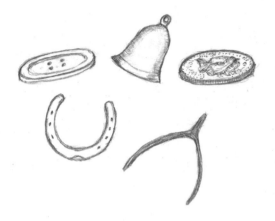

The congregation spilled out into the sunlight after the church service. Bells rang out in the cold air. The countryside still sparkled with frost.

Caroline bounced up to Joe. "Happy Christmas, see you later!" She put her hand over her mouth. "Oops! Forget I said that, will you?"

"Said what?"

Caroline jogged away, looking back at him. "Sorry, must dash, Mum's in a flap, lots of relations coming for lunch!"

At the mention of lunch Joe realised how hungry

he was. He started walking back to the car, eager to get home. It would have been great if Granny and Grandpa could have driven over from Birmingham for the day, but they were having what Dad called "an away match", staying with Dad's sister Steph and her children in Newcastle. Hopefully next year they'd all come to Newbridge Farm . . .

Still, Nellie had been invited to lunch, and she was almost family. In fact, she was better in many ways – somewhere between a wise but wonderfully eccentric grandmother and a best friend. Joe could tell Nellie things he couldn't tell anyone else, and only she knew about the horseshoe hidden in a box under his bed. She'd been there when Joe had dug it up in the field, and it was she who'd suggested making it into a wishing shoe, with a wish rolled up on a small piece of paper in each of the seven nail holes. Being a Romany, she knew about things like that. Perhaps she'd also guessed his wishes, although he'd only told her about the one for a dog.

Come to think of it, what *were* the others? He'd made them when he'd been homesick for Birmingham, just after Mum had fallen off Lady and ended up in hospital, before he'd started riding again. Yes, he remembered them now: *Get well Mum, Go home, Friends, Fortune, Good energy* and *England team.*

They'd been made only a few months ago, but

already things had changed. Mum had recovered, Newbridge Farm had become home, he had plenty of friends and life was good. Of course, a fortune would still be nice and it would be great to play for England, but those two had been long shots from the start.

All in all, he didn't think about his horseshoe so much nowadays. It was quite comforting to know it was there, though. Perhaps it was helping him all the time. Things had certainly got a whole lot better recently.

The smell of Christmas dinner cooking in the kitchen when they got home made Joe even hungrier. Mum said it wouldn't be ready for at least an hour, so he smuggled a large packet of crisps up to his bedroom, turned on his laptop, replied to some messages and downloaded some photos he'd taken onto Facebook. For his album cover, he chose a picture of Lightning looking straight at him, with frosty ground glistening all around her. He sat staring at it, munching a handful of crisps. It would make a brilliant Christmas card.

"Lunch time!" Mum called at last.

By the time Joe had eaten two helpings of roast turkey he was feeling rather full, but he definitely wanted to have some Christmas pudding because

Mum always hid silver charms in it. She'd used the same ones year after year, so they were tarnished with age, but that didn't matter. They were a link with the past – a family tradition.

Mum served the pudding carefully, making sure each person had a charm wrapped in waxed paper in their bowl before she handed it to them.

Emily unwrapped hers first. "A wishbone!" She closed her eyes tight. "Okay! I've made a wish. What have you got, Nellie?"

Nellie opened hers. "A bell."

"That means she'll be protected from evil, doesn't it, Mum?"

Mum nodded, and Nellie looked pleased. "Well, that's nice to know!"

"A bachelor's button, how appropriate," Dad said, holding it up for all to see. "Lucky for a man, unlucky for a lady."

Mum had something small and round. "A coin! How lovely – we can always do with more money."

All eyes turned to Joe. His charm had an unmistakable shape. He knew what it was before he removed the gluey paper pressed around it. "A lucky horseshoe."

Silence descended as they started eating, but with Emily around things never stayed silent for long. "Do Romanies believe in lucky charms?" she asked.

Nellie smiled. "Certainly, but we also believe you make your own luck in life."

Joe remembered her words about his horseshoe wishes: "The more help they get, the better they turn out."

"But what about fortune-telling? That says something's going to happen no matter what," Emily said, clearly pleased with herself for being so clever.

"Not necessarily," Nellie replied. "You see, we all have a life plan, but as life unfolds we experience infinite possibilities. Fortune-telling is much more complicated than people realise."

Emily shuffled her chair closer to Nellie's, and held out her palms. "Ooh, can you tell my fortune?"

Rusty, who'd been lying on the kitchen floor next to Joe's chair, got up and padded to the kitchen door. He stood with his head cocked on one side, listening. His tail wagged slowly, uncertainly.

Nellie took Emily's hands, and studied them with an air of intense concentration. "Let's see . . . I think that any moment now someone will knock on the door with a lovely surpr—"

There was a knock at the front door.

Rusty barked.

Emily looked down at her hands, then up at Nellie. "That's *amazing*!"

Nellie laughed gently. "I'm afraid I cheated a little

bit. Rusty could tell someone was coming."

"Oh." Emily looked disappointed and relieved at the same time. Joe knew how she felt. It would have been really spooky if Nellie had been that good at predicting the future.

"Come on, Emily, we'd better go and see who it is," Mum said, getting up from the table. Joe saw her catch Dad's eye, and they grinned at each other. What were they up to?

They all followed Mum to the front door. Rusty pushed past, barking and wagging his tail enthusiastically. It must be someone he knows, Joe thought. He remembered the conversation in the pub, Caroline's greeting outside church, the clean stable, and Emily's grooming kit. Of course! Why hadn't he guessed before?

Mum opened the door.

"*We wish you a merry Christmas, we wish you a merry—*" Caroline sang.

Emily interrupted her with a cry of "Treacle!" She rushed forwards to hug him.

The little pony stood beside Caroline, unfazed by the commotion, the pretend reindeer antlers attached to his tinsel-covered head collar at a jaunty angle, having been knocked out of place by Emily.

"Guess what, darling?" Mum said to Emily. "Caroline has very kindly said you can borrow Treacle!"

"What? Keep him here?"

"Yes, and treat him like your own pony, although he'll be going back to Lucketts Farm for Angus to ride when he's old enough."

"Oh!" Emily looked as if she'd burst with excitement. "But how did you know? That was my wish – my Christmas pudding wish – and it's come true! Oh, thank you!" She hugged Treacle again, and this time the antlers flopped over his eyes.

Chapter 6

J oe was sure Emily would soon get bored with the hard work of looking after a pony, but she proved him wrong. Throughout the rest of the Christmas holidays she spent every moment she could with Treacle, mucking out his stable, grooming him, cleaning his tack, riding or just admiring him with a dreamy look on her face.

With Treacle to give her confidence, her riding improved so that she no longer had to be on the leading rein if they went out for hacks with Chris and Caroline, and before long she was galloping along with the rest of them, balanced perfectly in the saddle as if she'd been riding all her life.

Chris made no secret of how impressed he was by Emily's progress and how well Treacle went for her. Joe felt sorry for Caroline when Chris said things like that. He could tell it was hard for her to see Emily bonding easily with the pony she'd called her own for so many years. The situation wasn't helped by the fact that Minstrel, Simon's old pony, was proving to be quite a handful.

"He's got two speeds: stop and go," Caroline muttered as Minstrel cantered sideways up the road with his head tucked into his chest while everyone else walked home on a loose rein. He looked very impressive, like a fiery dressage pony, but Joe felt glad he wasn't riding him.

"Try to relax and give him his head a bit more," Chris suggested.

"I've tried that, but he just charges off!" Caroline shouted over her shoulder.

Chris dropped back to ride alongside Joe. "Simon always rides his ponies flat out, that's the trouble. Minstrel doesn't know walking's allowed. He's fine at mounted games because he understands what he's supposed to be doing, but he thinks everything's a race now. Poor Caroline – it's always difficult changing ponies."

Especially when your old one has been such a good friend and you see him nearly every day, Joe said to himself. He couldn't imagine letting anyone else have Lightning, but in the back of his mind he knew that before long he'd grow out of her. Then what? He'd rather not think about it.

The rest of the holidays flew by. There were good times, like the New Year's Eve party in The Ewe and Lamb, and not so good times, like Emily's birthday on the third of January.

It was on Emily's birthday that Joe realised the tables had turned. She was now considered to be the horsey one of the family – the one who would go far in the riding world. Most of her presents were horse-themed, including a pink and purple turnout rug with matching head collar, a tweed hacking jacket and a year's subscription to the Bellsham Vale branch of the Pony Club. Over breakfast she treated Mum, Dad and Joe to a recital of the entire Pony Club fixtures list for the coming year, interspersed with comments about what she and Treacle were going to do and what Treacle would say about it all.

Joe escaped outside as soon as he could. Emily had stolen the limelight, as usual. Riding was his hobby – more than a hobby, actually. He'd been the trailblazer and Emily had strolled into the opening he'd made. He'd spent hours riding Lady and leading Lightning, gradually building Lady's trust and helping Lightning's feet heal. Although he'd enjoyed it, getting his pony fit enough to ride had involved a lot of work. But now Emily had been given the whole thing on a plate, including Caroline's perfect pony.

"Emily may have Treacle, but Lightning's mine," Joe said out loud. "Nothing will ever change that." He picked up a dung fork and started mucking out his pony's stable furiously.

Aikido lessons in Bellsham on Saturday afternoons started again with the new school term. Joe loved aikido, especially because all his best friends – Martin, Caroline, Darren and Spike – were in the same class. Their teacher, Sensei Radford, had a knack of getting his pupils to see life from a different angle. At the end of the lesson he always gathered them together for a talk about something.

"*Osu,*" Sensei Radford said. "We say it when we walk into the dojo and when we're practising aikido, but what does it mean? Yes, Spike?"

"I will do my best?"

"That's right. *Osu* literally means to push to the limits of endurance and persevere, or to do the best you can. It is of vital importance to do your absolute best, no matter what. Life is full of many paths we can take, and along each path there are decisions to be made. We all lead different lives, with different paths to choose and challenges to face, but we must take ownership of the life we've been given and make the most of it. Each one of us must be the best we can be."

Joe remembered what Nellie had said at Christmas lunch: "We all have a life plan, but as life unfolds we experience infinite possibilities . . ."

"Who can name the three Rs?" Sensei Radford asked.

Joe put up his hand. With parents who were teachers, he could hardly fail to know. "Reading, writing and arithmetic."

"As with so many questions in life, there's more than one right answer," Sensei Radford said, smiling at him. "The answer I had in mind was the Dalai Lama's: respect for self, respect for others and responsibility for all your actions." He counted each one off on his fingers as he said it, and then looked up at his class. "As you all know, aikido was originally a Japanese martial art taught to Samurai warriors, who were expected to fight to the death. I most definitely don't want any of you to hurt anybody, so why am I teaching it to you?"

There was a pause.

"Because aikido helps us believe in ourselves and be true to our inner self so we can live our lives in a positive, productive way. It teaches us to be confident in our abilities and aware of our limitations, and it emphasises the importance of consideration towards others. In short, aikido teaches us *responsibility*." Sensei Radford paused.

Joe caught his intense gaze. It felt like a physical force.

"Accepting responsibility is incredibly liberating," Sensei Radford continued. "In aikido, and in life, you are responsible for everything you do. *You own your life*. You shouldn't be bothered about what other people are doing, or how your life measures up against theirs. Just be true to yourself. Do what you feel is right. Be the best you can possibly be. *Osu*."

"*Osu*," they replied.

"You're very quiet, Joe," Caroline said as they walked down the steps of the dojo. "Is everything okay?"

"Yes, fine," Joe replied. "I was just thinking."

"About what Sensei Radford said?"

"Yes, sort of. I mean, it's made me decide something."

Caroline looked at him quizzically.

He didn't really want to tell her, especially with

Martin and Spike within hearing distance. "It's nothing important."

"Oh yes it is! Come on, you can tell me." She pulled her glossy brown hair behind her ear. "Whisper it."

"Promise you won't laugh?"

Caroline nodded.

Joe moved as close as he dared and said in a half-whisper, "I'm going to use my Christmas money to join the Pony Club."

Chapter 7

"You're full of surprises," Mum said when Joe asked her to fill in the parental consent part of the Pony Club membership application form.

"Why is it so surprising?" Joe asked.

"Well, you always enjoy doing the sorts of things boys do – aikido, football and fishing, for instance."

"And why shouldn't riding be the sort of thing boys do?"

Mum hesitated.

"What about the Olympics? Plenty of men rode

in that," Joe said. "And how about jockeys? They're nearly all men."

"You're absolutely right," Mum replied. "I think it's great you want to join the Pony Club. Don't worry about raiding your savings. Dad and I will pay. Call it a late Christmas present."

"Thanks, Mum. I need to send everything off as soon as possible, though. Caroline says the mounted games team trials are in February."

Mum looked worried. "I know you did well at the Christmas rally, but the competition for a place in the team will be pretty fierce, I expect, so please don't raise your hopes too high. Why not wait until next year, when you'll be much more experienced?"

"Because I may have grown out of Lightning by then. This could be my only chance. I've got to give it a go, at least."

Mum smiled. "Good for you."

Joe couldn't really explain why getting into the mounted games team had become so important to him. At the Christmas rally he'd discovered the excitement of riding his pony at speed, the satisfaction of getting a difficult manoeuvre right, the thrill of people cheering him on and the pleasure of winning, but there was more to it than that. He'd also experienced a connection with his pony that until then he'd never have believed possible – a feeling they were inseparable, thinking and acting as one. It was the best feeling in the world. Lightning obviously loved mounted games as much as he did; he wanted to get into the team for her sake as well as his.

With only a few weeks and limited daylight in which to practise before the team trials, every opportunity was precious. There was so much to learn. Joe could hardly wait until his first training session with Chris in the indoor school at Lucketts Farm the following weekend.

As soon as he woke on Sunday morning, Joe could tell something had happened. The room was much lighter than usual and he felt an eerie stillness in the air.

He got up and shuffled to the window with his duvet huddled around him for warmth.

Rusty jumped around, barking with excitement.

"Lie down!" Joe said. "I'll take you out in a minute."

Snow! It really *had* snowed, too. Not half-hearted city slush, but great billowy piles of the stuff. Snow clung to everything, from twigs to rooftops. Even in the semi-darkness, it radiated white light. Plump snowflakes tumbled from the leaden sky, settling invisibly. Layer upon layer.

The initial thrill Joe had felt turned into frustration as he remembered what was supposed to be happening that day. They wouldn't be able to get up to Lucketts Farm in this weather – no way.

The cold spell lasted for nearly two weeks. *Spell* described it well, Joe thought. Water turned rock-solid in troughs and buckets, and the ground transformed into a treacherous mixture of snowdrifts and packed ice that mapped the daily cycle of activity at the farm. It was impossible to ride in such conditions. Fresh falls of snow alternated with freezing, clear snaps. The council gave up trying to keep every road open, so Newbridge Farm became cut off. If Joe hadn't been so worried about not being able to ride Lightning he would have been delighted about the unexpected holiday. His days were spent tobogganing with friends, building giant snowmen and going on intrepid dog-walks through the frozen countryside. Rusty's favourite game was to dive head-first into a drift, dig like crazy, emerge covered in snow and shake it all off. He came back from walks wet but incredibly clean.

The snow disappeared almost as quickly as it had

come, leaving drab sogginess in its wake, and life returned to normal.

With the team trials looming there was no time to lose. Joe started to ride Lightning again as soon as it was safe. She was particularly bouncy after her time off, and sweated up quickly. Joe wondered about getting her winter coat clipped, but didn't know how to go about it. He couldn't ask Chris for yet another favour. Perhaps he'd ask if he knew of anyone who clipped horses. Yes, that would be the best thing to do. He'd ask him on Sunday morning, when they were going to have their long-awaited training session in the indoor school. Caroline had persuaded Emily to try for the junior team on Treacle, so she was going to join in too. Joe was pleased they'd all be practising together, but part of him wished Emily would get into something different, like dressage or show jumping.

"Okay, we haven't got much time, so what do you want to learn?" Chris asked as they entered the indoor school.

"Vaulting," Joe said.

"Ooh, yes," Emily agreed.

"Good idea. Caroline, come and give us a demonstration," Chris said.

Caroline rode Minstrel forwards, jumped off and then leapt back on again in one easy movement.

"How d'you do that?" Joe asked.

"I don't know, really. I've been doing it for so long I don't have to think about it. In fact, if I thought about it I probably wouldn't be able to do it," she replied.

Chris smiled at Joe reassuringly. "Don't worry, I'll come and help you."

Emily learned to vault from a standstill at the second time of trying, just like that, and proceeded to master the art when Treacle was trotting, then cantering. Once she'd got the knack, she showed off her new skill at every possible opportunity.

"It's easier the faster you go, Joe!" she said. "Don't think too much about it – just do it!"

Joe wished he could practise without Caroline, Emily and Chris watching. "Stand still," he told Lightning unnecessarily as she remained motionless, patiently waiting for him to get on so they could start doing something interesting. He stood by her shoulder, facing her tail, and put his left hand on the pommel of the saddle, as Chris had taught him to. "One, two, three," he said under his breath, going through the motions in his mind: step back on right leg, spring forward off left leg and swing right leg over saddle, hooking it over the cantle . . . His left leg just wouldn't spring enough to get his right leg over the saddle. His pony was too tall, the back of the saddle was too high, the surface of the school was too soft – there had to be *some* good reason why he couldn't get the hang of it.

He became more disheartened with each failure, despite well-meaning remarks from Chris like, "Oh, nearly!"

Eventually Chris said, "Don't worry, Joe. It can take people ages to learn. I bet once you've got it you'll wonder why you ever found it difficult."

"Did you see that girl in the zone finals last year? She never vaulted on. Always used a stirrup," Caroline said, trying to cheer him up.

Chris picked a couple of batons out of a bucket. "Yes, it really isn't the end of the world if you can't vault, as long as you get on quickly. Anyway, we won't worry about that now. Let's concentrate on some of the other things you'll need to know for the team trials, like the correct way to hold a baton."

Emily looked amazed. "You mean there's even a right and wrong way to hold one of those?"

"Absolutely," Chris replied. "And a correct way to do a changeover."

"In fact," Caroline added, "races are often lost because batons are dropped or not handed over properly."

Chris held the baton up. It was green in the middle and black at each end. "Okay, first rule: all changeovers must take place with both the incoming and outgoing pony behind the line. Even one hoof over the line could mean elimination. Second rule: always pass right hand to right hand. Third rule: the outgoing rider holds his, or her, hand out and keeps it still so the incoming rider can place the baton directly into their hand. The last rider takes it over the line." He held the baton at its centre. "When you're riding, it's safest to hold it like this, but just before the changeover it's a good idea to tap the end on your thigh or chest, like so," he tapped the baton on his leg so his hand shifted to one end. "That way, the next rider will find it easier to grasp." He handed the baton to Emily, who took it with a self-conscious grin, and tapped it expertly on her leg so her hand slid to one end.

They pretended they were a team doing a bending race, so they could practise handing over the baton. Then they went through some other races. Caroline's pony, Minstrel, became so wound up that he kept running backwards when he saw another pony approaching.

Red in the face, she turned to Chris. "He did this at the Christmas rally too! I don't know how to stop him." She glanced longingly at Treacle, who hadn't put a foot wrong during the entire session.

"Don't get stressed, or he'll pick up on it and become even more excited," Chris said. "I seem to remember Simon used to have the same problem, so he held Minstrel well behind the line and drove him forwards as the incoming pony approached. You see, it's more difficult for a pony to go backwards if he's already going forwards."

Caroline tried what Chris suggested.

"See? Much better," Chris said. "But you'll have to time the changeover just right or he'll be over the line before you've got the baton." He turned to Joe and Emily. "Groom Lightning and Treacle well tonight, and I'll drop in to clip them tomorrow morning, if you like. Ask your mum to leave them in their stables. I'll just give them trace clips."

"Great, thanks." Joe paused. "What's a trace clip?"

"Hairs on the belly and the underside of the neck are removed, so the pony doesn't sweat so much but it still has some protection from cold weather." Chris looked from Joe to Emily and back again. "Have they got rugs?"

They both nodded.

"Good. And I know it's difficult to ride when you've been at school, because it gets dark so early and there's homework to do, but you're welcome to put in some practice up here in the evenings if you've got time. The team trials are only a week away, remember."

No chance of forgetting, Joe thought. I can't think of anything else at the moment.

Chapter 8

"What on earth are you doing?" Mum asked as she walked into the sitting room that afternoon.

Joe jumped off the back of the sofa. "Nothing."

"Doesn't look like nothing to me."

He'd have to say, however daft it sounded. "Okay, I was trying to practise vaulting, that's all. Chris suggested using the back of a sofa or a gate as a pretend horse. The sofa's lower and it's got padding, so I thought I'd start on that."

"Oh. Can't you use something else?"

"No, this is perfect, and I'm really getting the hang of it now. Look!" Joe gripped the head rest with his left hand, sprang from his right leg to his left and threw his right leg over. The sofa tipped slightly as he landed astride, then juddered to an upright position again.

"I think you'd better stop right there," Mum said. "Your pony's out in the stable. Go and practise on her."

"I thought she needed some time off. She was getting fed up with me this morning."

"She's probably forgiven you by now," Mum said. "You'll have to start vaulting on her soon. The team trials are next Sunday, aren't they?"

Thanks for reminding me, Joe thought, and went outside.

The ponies had been moved to the long barn a few days ago, and Joe still couldn't get used to seeing them in their smart new home. The barn had been repaired, a concrete floor had been laid and ten stables had been installed, with a central passageway running through the middle and an improvised tack room and feed shed at the far end.

The stable walls were made from pre-fabricated sections. The sides had wood below and steel bars above, so that the horses were able to see each other but not make physical contact. The front sections were the same, but with a split door in the middle and a really cool feed bin which swung all the way round so you could feed each horse from the passageway without entering the stable – especially useful for horses like ET who became anxious at meal times.

ET wasn't there – not for the moment, anyway – and that took some getting used to as well. Her owner had decided to put her in foal, so she'd gone off to a thoroughbred stud for a while. The thought of ET with a beautiful spindly-legged foal running by her side made Joe feel all happy inside. In the long term he wanted time to whizz by so next year would come quickly, but for the next week he wanted it to go slowly so he'd be able to master vaulting before the team trials.

Lightning had the first stable on the left. Treacle was next door and Lady was opposite. The rest of the barn was empty, but with any luck it wouldn't be for long. Mum was creating a Hidden Horseshoe website, and she'd just been interviewed about the horse sanctuary by a well-known equestrian magazine. They'd been particularly interested in Lightning's recovery from lameness and Chris' hoof rehabilitation methods. Mum had high hopes that the article would generate a lot of business.

Although Lightning was too well-mannered to turn away or pin her ears back when Joe tacked her up for the second time that day, he knew her well enough to see she wasn't happy. Her nostrils were pinched and her chin was rigid when he put the bit in her mouth.

Joe checked the girth and led Lighting out into the passageway. "Stand," he said as he grabbed hold of the front of the saddle. Then he took three deep breaths, concentrated hard and, with a tremendous effort, jumped.

Result! Well, sort of . . . He managed to hook his leg over the cantle, and he clung on like a monkey as he gradually hauled himself upright. At last, exhausted, he was on.

Lightning shifted her weight uncomfortably and swished her tail in disapproval.

He stroked her neck. "I know this isn't much fun for you at the moment, but I will get better, I promise, and then we'll have some fun. I want to become as good as you are at mounted games, but we've got to do it together. With your help I'll try to be the best I can be." The word *Osu* popped into his mind, and he remembered what had happened yesterday in aikido.

Sensei Radford had called him to the front of the class. "I want you to concentrate all your thoughts into the top of your head," he'd said.

Joe had concentrated so hard that his scalp had

tingled. Perhaps that was the point of the exercise.

"Now, I'm going to give you a light push on your shoulder."

Joe had toppled backwards even though Sensei Radford hadn't pushed hard.

"It's easy to make someone off-balance when they're concentrating on their head," Sensei Radford had said. "Now I'd like you to focus your mind on a place right in the centre of yourself, just below your belly button, in the middle of your pelvis."

Joe had done his best to concentrate on that, although it seemed a funny thing to do.

"Okay, I'm going to use the same amount of force on your shoulder again."

The push on his shoulder had felt feeble that time. In fact, Sensei Radford had only been able to shift him with a hard push. Joe had never felt so balanced and in control of himself. It had seemed like a magic trick.

"See? By coordinating the power of your mind and body you can achieve great things. When your mind is concentrating on your true centre of balance it becomes your centre of power. As you become better at aikido you will learn to concentrate power at your core so you can direct it to your limbs."

That's the answer! Joe said to himself. Even Caroline finds it hard to vault on if she thinks too much about it; perhaps that's where I've been going wrong; I've been concentrating on the instructions in my head rather than the energy in my body.

With new-found enthusiasm, Joe dismounted, gripped the front of the saddle and tried to concentrate on the power in his body. He imagined he was in the saddle almost before he landed there – it was as if the power inside him was leaping ahead, showing the way. Wow! He'd done it!

Perhaps it was a fluke.

He got off, and tried again. He'd try to do it more gently, more fluently . . .

Amazing! The thrill of success coursed through his body, fuelling him. Soon he was landing softly in the saddle every time and wondering why he'd ever found vaulting so difficult.

Lightning stopped looking unhappy and anxious. In fact, she looked like Joe felt – relieved that he'd finally got it.

On Mondays Joe had football practice after school and on Wednesday he played in a match, but on Tuesday and Thursday he and Emily took their ponies up to Lucketts Farm and practised mounted games with Caroline.

"Brilliant! You can do it! I knew you would," she

exclaimed when she saw him vault on Lightning the first time. "Woo-hoo! Prince Philip Cup, here we come!"

Joe grinned, thrilled by her reaction, and patted Lightning's neck. "I've still got to learn how to vault on when she's moving, though," he said.

"Don't worry, Chris said he'd come and help us have a final training session on Friday."

"How about Saturday? There'll be time before aikido. Can't we practise then as well?"

"Afraid not. We're all going point-to-pointing, so everything will be locked up for the day."

On Friday, Chris taught Joe how to vault on Lightning when she was moving.

It took a lot of nerve to begin with. Joe had to run beside Lightning, with his left hand up her mane and his right hand gripping the right side of the saddle by the pommel, then do a two-footed jump forwards – just in front of her shoulder – and spring up and over into the saddle. Once or twice he forgot to stay facing forwards and ended up belly-flopping into the saddle, but he soon got the hang of it. Emily had been right: vaulting on Lightning when she was moving was much easier because he could use her forward motion to lift himself up.

Fired with enthusiasm and undaunted by drizzly rain, Joe and Emily practised different races in a field at Newbridge Farm on Saturday. They used upturned buckets, sticks, ice cream containers and odd socks scrunched into balls as equipment.

By the evening Joe felt ready for the team trials. Excitement, more than anxiety, disturbed his sleep that night.

Chapter 9

A select bunch of athletic-looking riders on eager ponies gathered in the massive indoor arena at the equestrian centre near Bellsham that had been hired for the trials. Some were already doing warm-up exercises and practising various moves with casual self-confidence when Joe rode in.

He took a deep breath. Focus your energy, stay calm, he told himself.

It worked. Bending, his favourite race, went really well. Lightning weaved in and out of the poles on auto-pilot while he sat tight and remembered how to hand over the baton. Job done.

In the mug race his mug slipped off the pole, but he soon jumped off, picked it up and vaulted on again like a pro.

He even remembered to turn the flag over so the next person could take it from him easily in the flag race. Lightning seemed to know exactly what to do in the pyramid race, and they excelled in the individual sack race. Joe had always been good at sack races. Things were going well.

Maria, Simon's mum, was in charge. She had a horsey voice – sort of posh and rather bossy, with raspy undertones. The helpers, including Chris, rushed to oblige whenever she asked them to do something, like setting up lines of upturned plastic containers for a stepping stone race.

This'll be good fun, Joe thought as he watched them. He knew what he'd have to do because he'd looked up the rules on a mounted games internet site. In his mind he ran through it: gallop up to the stepping stones, dismount, run over them leading Lightning to one side, vault on and race to the far end. It'd be a good chance to show off his vaulting-at-speed skills.

Chris, who'd been setting up the line furthest away from Joe, caught his attention with a wave and then did a funny mime of dismounting and running with his right hand up in the air, presumably holding on to an imaginary horse.

He's telling me I've got to run across the stepping stones, Joe thought. He grinned and did a thumbs-up sign to let him know he understood.

Chris gave Joe a thumbs-up with both hands before joining the other helpers by the side of the arena.

Maria strode out in front of the riders. "Okay, folks! This is the final race. Can I have Simon, Caroline, Sarah, Ali, Joe and Hattie in the first line-up, please!" She took up her position as starter – standing at the side of the arena, about a third of the way up so everyone could see the white flag raised above her head.

Joe took his place between two grey ponies ridden by Ali and Hattie, and felt Lightning tremble with anticipation as they waited for the flag to go down.

"Go!" Joe told Lightning, but she'd seen the flag too and had already surged forwards. He could see the stepping stones coming up fast. Fumbling with his reins, he tried to steady her by sitting up straight. Good pony! She checked to a trot, obviously thinking that was slow enough. Joe kicked his feet out of the stirrups, grabbed hold of the pommel with his right hand, flung his leg over the back of the saddle, dropped down to the ground, felt his legs crumple underneath him and fell flat on his face.

Chris delivered them to Newbridge Farm so Joe wouldn't have far to walk.

"How did you get on?" Mum asked as they scrambled down from the horse lorry. She looked at Joe. "Oh dear! What happened to you?"

"Joe face-planted," Emily said before Joe could explain.

"I beg your pardon?" Mum replied.

"He fell flat on his face in the stepping stones race. It wasn't really his fault, 'cos nobody had told him how to get off a moving pony. He should have jumped off facing forwards and hit the ground running at the same speed as Lightning, you see." Emily thought for a moment. "*Actually*, Chris tried to show him what to do just before the race, but—"

Joe glowered at her.

"But the good news," she said quickly, "is that we're all in the team!"

"All three of you?" Mum exclaimed.

"Not exactly. Caroline and I are in the senior team and Emily's with the juniors," Joe said.

"But Treacle was so good today that I may be needed as a reserve for the senior team as well," Emily squeaked. "Ali's the reserve, but her pony goes lame sometimes so I'm on emergency standby."

Poised to save the world, Joe thought wryly.

"Well done all of you," Mum said. She hugged Emily and then moved to hug Joe.

"Ouch," he said. His whole body felt bruised.

"Oh! Sorry, darling. Do you think you ought to be checked out by a doctor?"

"It's okay," Emily said. "Maria's a physio-terrorist—"

Mum laughed. "I think you mean *physiotherapist*."

"Yes, that's right. She says Joe's grazed his face and twisted his knee but it isn't serious or anything. She said something about rice, but I didn't understand that bit."

"R.I.C.E. It stands for rest, ice, compression and elevation." Mum looked at Joe. "We'll have to sit you down with your leg in the air and a pack of frozen peas on your knee this evening."

Joe shivered. "No thanks."

Mum looked concerned. "Poor old you. Go and warm yourself up in the kitchen. I'll tuck Lightning up for the night, if you like."

"Thanks, Mum. She was great – tried her heart out. I was the one who mucked everything up."

Mum smiled. "Don't be too hard on yourself; Maria's chosen you for the team, remember, so you can't have done that badly. Everyone makes mistakes sometimes, and it's far better to make them now than in the Prince Philip Cup final."

"Steady on," Joe replied. "We haven't got through the first round yet."

But as he sat drinking hot chocolate by the kitchen range, he allowed himself to dream . . .

Chapter 10

Joe soon recovered from his fall, which was just as well because the second half of the spring term became really busy. His football team at school was doing well and their teacher wanted to fit in more training and matches on Saturdays, which often clashed with aikido. Also, he had an increasing number of mounted games practice sessions and competitions in preparation for the area competition in April. Reluctantly, he decided to give up aikido for the time being. Sensei Radford was very understanding, and told Joe he'd be welcome back any time.

Luckily it was nearly the end of the school football season, so Joe didn't have to choose between football and mounted games. If he had, mounted games would have won. He'd been given the chance of a lifetime with Lightning, and he wasn't going to waste it.

Everyone kept saying what an amazing pony he had, but he didn't need to be told – he was the one who rode her, after all. He knew how she watched the flag and accelerated away the moment it was down; how she memorised the rules of each game and helped him every step of the way; how it felt to be completely in tune with another living being. Nothing matched up to that.

"I wonder who taught her to be so good at games," he said to Nellie as they led the ponies in from the field one day at the beginning of the Easter holidays. "I'd love to know more about her."

"Have you looked at her passport?" Nellie asked. "Her previous owners should be recorded there, along with their addresses. You could write to them."

"Of course! You're a genius!"

Nellie looked pleased. "Why, thank you, kind sir," she joked, and gave a little bow. "Glad to be of service."

That evening he asked Mum for Lightning's passport.

"Why do you want it?" she asked. "The practice tomorrow is at Lucketts, isn't it? You only need to take it with you when you're transporting her somewhere."

"I know that," Joe replied. "I want to contact her previous owners – try to find out about her past."

"What a good idea," Mum said, handing him the passport. "Good luck."

Joe took it to his room, sat down at the desk and thumbed through the pages. He'd never really taken much interest in it before. Chris was always grumbling about horse passports, saying they were a waste of time and money because there were so many different organisations selling them and endless opportunities for fraud . . . Passports were yet another example of bureaucracy gone mad, he said.

Well, they might be useful after all, Joe thought as he came to a page titled *Details Of Ownership And Endorsement Of Acceptance By Owners (Or Appointed Agents)*. Three names and addresses were listed. The first was somebody called Moira Fraser from a place called Auchterarder in Scotland, the second was a Mr DM James from somewhere near Hastings in Sussex and the third was Mum. Lightning had certainly travelled around a lot. Judging by the dates, some former owners seemed to be missing from the records – including the person who'd sold them Lady and Lightning.

Joe looked at the front of the passport to confirm when Lightning was born, and found another name and address under the heading *Breeder: Diana Watson-Clarke, Westerclose Farm, near Winchester, Hampshire.* Pity there were no email addresses or telephone numbers. He'd have to write three letters.

He studied the details on the passport. Lightning's registered name was Westerclose Lightning. She was now fourteen years old. Her mother was called Westerclose Perfect Storm and her father was Bluestone Flash.

Hence Lightning, Joe said to himself as he settled down to write his letters.

Mum posted them first class when she went shopping in Bellsham the following day.

Joe estimated it would take about four days for a reply to arrive. At least there'd be plenty of fun stuff going on to keep him busy – riding, being with Rusty and hanging out with his mates, especially Martin.

Thanks to Martin, Joe had become really keen on fishing. Whenever they could they went to a huge lake stocked with brown trout belonging to a farmer who was a regular in The Ewe and Lamb.

Joe had never had a friend quite like Martin before. With others there'd always been an edge – a feeling that friendship was conditional in some way – but Martin's friendship came with a lifetime guarantee and an endless supply of free jokes.

"What did the fish say when it ran into a brick wall?" he asked as they sat by the side of the lake. It was their first fishing expedition of the holidays.

Joe thought for a moment. "Don't know."

"Dam!" Martin said triumphantly.

"That's terrible! Okay then, what's the difference between a fish and a piano?"

"Easy. You can't tuna fish." Martin's line went taut, and he started reeling in his first catch of the day.

Joe looked on with envy as he scooped a large trout into his net. "How come you always catch more than I do?"

Martin shrugged. "I've learned to see things from a fish's point of view, I suppose. It's like Sensei Radford was saying yesterday."

"Oh? I wasn't there, remember. I had games practice."

"He said that seeing things from the other person's point of view is vital in aikido, so you get to know instinctively what they're going to do. Well, that got me thinking, because trying to imagine what I'd do if I were a fish has definitely made me better at fishing."

Joe nodded. "It's the same with horses. If you see

things from their point of view it makes life a whole lot easier." He got up, yawned and stretched.

Rusty, who'd been dozing peacefully by Joe's side, got up and stretched too. Then he trotted over to Joe's rucksack and looked at it intently, as if it might move at any second.

Joe laughed. "It's not difficult to see life from your point of view, is it Rusty? Everything revolves around food for you!"

A week passed, but there were no replies to Joe's letters.

ET came back from the stud with a certificate confirming she was in foal, which was a huge relief because if she hadn't managed to get in foal her owner would have sold her. Less good news was that she'd started box-walking again and she had infected scabs on her legs.

"You'd have thought they'd have noticed her mud fever and done something about it," Joe said to Nellie as they stood looking at ET pacing around her stable. "Why didn't they wash her legs off every evening and dry them with a towel, like we do?"

"Didn't have me breathing down their necks, telling them what to do," Nellie said. She sighed. "Laziness is a large part of it, I expect. People turn a blind eye in these large places – think it's somebody else's problem."

ET stood still for a moment, with her head over the door.

Joe stroked her neck and felt a thrill as he imagined the invisible new life developing inside her. "Don't worry, we'll look after you. You're home now."

A few days later, a letter arrived for Joe. The writing was spidery and rather shaky. The envelope was stamped with a Winchester postmark. He opened it, and read:

Dear Mr Williams,

Thank you for your letter.

I'm afraid my wife, Diana, died a couple of years ago. The ponies were her 'babies', so to speak, and I had little to do with that side of things. I do remember a mare called Storm. She was one of Diana's favourites.

I'm sorry that I can't help you further, but I wish you every success with your pony. Diana would be delighted that Lightning has found a loving home.

Yours sincerely,

Patrick Watson-Clarke

Joe handed the letter to Mum, who was waiting expectantly.

She read it and said, "It was nice of him to reply, wasn't it? You never know, the others may write soon."

"Doubt it," Joe said.

"Well, if they don't, at least you tried," Mum said in a cheery voice.

Easter Day came and went. No more letters arrived for Joe, but he hardly had time to wonder about Lightning's past now. All his thoughts were focussed on the future and the area competition.

Chapter 11

Rain splattered against the windscreen. The wipers swept to and fro, squeaking against the glass. The heater puffed warm, humid air around the lorry cab, adding a dull humming noise to the purr of the engine and the swish of tyres on the wet motorway.

Joe sat squashed between Emily and the door. He could feel her body jiggling around. "Sit still, will you?" he whispered.

"I can't," she whispered back. "Nervous. Aren't you?"

"No." I don't know what you're worried about – you're only the reserve, he thought.

She grinned. "Don't believe you. Why didn't you eat any breakfast?"

"Wasn't hungry."

"You're always hungry!"

"Sshhh!" Joe's stomach writhed and his nerves crackled. They'd been in the lorry for nearly two hours. Not long now . . .

"Can we stop at the next service station, Tracey? I think I need the loo," Emily said.

Joe had to admit Emily had her uses. He'd been too embarrassed to ask.

The area competition took place in a huge field not far from the motorway. Joe had never seen so many ponies, people and lorries.

Tracey seemed to know exactly where to park. No sooner had she switched off the engine than Maria was tapping on the window of the lorry, holding out some green bibs and numnahs. Tracey opened the door. Cold, damp air rushed into the fuggy cab.

"Bit of a hiccup," Maria said cheerfully. "Ted's lame, so Ali can't come. Sorry to spring this on you, Emily, but could you possibly ride in the team?"

Joe felt Emily tense beside him. She'd only been

made reserve last week because Hattie's family had moved house suddenly, and now she was being asked to ride in the all-important area competition. Talk about being thrown in at the deep end, Joe thought.

"Super," Maria said, although Emily hadn't said a word. "So it'll be Simon on Rolo, Sarah on Flicka, Joe on Lightning, Caroline on Minstrel and you on Treacle today. Okay?"

"Um, okay," she said, and then giggled nervously.

Joe instinctively put his arm around her and gave her a hug. "You'll be fine," he said. "Treacle will look after you."

An easterly wind swept across the vast field, stealing the warmth from their bodies as they sat on their ponies in their jods and Pony Club sweatshirts, waiting for the bending race to begin. Joe longed for the coat he'd left in the lorry, but coats weren't allowed. His teeth chattered with cold. He glanced at Emily. She caught his eye and smiled shakily with colourless lips. He smiled back, feeling a rush of admiration for his little sister. If she could stick this out, so could he.

Caroline went first, followed by Emily. Treacle whipped between the poles, turned sharply at the far end and galloped flat-out towards Joe.

He held out a numb hand and waited to grip the baton. "Go!" Lightning exploded into action. Joe had never known her this fast. The end pole approached. Sit up, neck-rein, lean . . . He felt a jolt – like the slipping, tripping, falling sensation he sometimes had just before going to sleep – and he heard the spectators fall silent, then gasp. He grabbed the pommel of the saddle as Lightning's body fell away beneath him. The crowd went "Ahh!" and he felt her lurch up again. Legs gathered underneath her once more, she accelerated down the line of poles towards the waiting ponies. Just in time, Joe remembered to tap the baton on his leg so Sarah would be able to hold it easily.

They were still in the lead, despite Lightning losing her footing. Joe knew he'd have to be careful in the other races; she didn't have shoes, so she couldn't have studs to stop her from slipping on the wet ground.

Sarah was in second place as she handed the baton to Simon, but bending was Rolo's speciality. He soon regained the lead, and thundered over the finish line a pole's length ahead of everyone else. They'd won the first race of the competition!

They came first in the pyramid race too. What a great start! Joe and his team mates grinned and gave each other high fives.

The ball and cone race didn't go so well. Caroline's ball toppled off her cone. She had to get off to pick it up. Minstrel charged after the other ponies as they overtook, and Caroline only just managed to vault on in time. They came fourth. It was a shock; they'd become used to winning.

Joe and Sarah made mistakes in the litter race, and the team came third. Had they lost their winning streak? But then, thank goodness, they were back on form in the quoits and cone – first place, and second in the tyre race. The excitement grew as each race whizzed by . . . They were up with the front-runners again!

Stepping stones next. After his accident at the team trials Joe was nervous, but he needn't have worried. Lightning slowed at just the right moment, matched him step for step as he ran across the stones and accelerated away when he vaulted on again. At the end of the race they were lying in second place, with two points between them and the leaders.

The final contest was the five flag. The Bellsham Vale was in front as Joe crossed the line, and it was still in the lead when Caroline handed over to Emily, but two other teams weren't far behind and Treacle wasn't as fast as some of the larger ponies. It looked as if they wouldn't win after all, but Simon and Rolo saved the day with a spectacularly fast run.

They'd won!

The early start, tedious journey, nerves and cold weather were all forgotten as Joe pinned a first rosette to Lightning's bridle. He caught Emily's eye, and grinned.

She grinned back and gave Treacle a quick hug.

He couldn't help feeling proud of her . . . And a tiny bit jealous at her instant success, but he'd have to deal with that.

As soon as all the rosettes had been handed out, the Bellsham Vale team set off for a lap of honour around the arena. Treacle, Lightning and Minstrel galloped side by side – ears forward, toes pointed and necks arched – thoroughly enjoying themselves.

Joe wondered whether they realised they'd come first. Perhaps they even knew they'd be going to the zone finals in June. He was coming to the conclusion that horses understood much more than most people gave them credit for.

Chapter 12

The Hidden Horseshoe Sanctuary was now open for business, with state-of-the-art stabling and stock-proof fields. Mum started advertising, and before long they had some new residents: Otto, Humphrey, Bubble and Squeak.

Otto was a beautiful liver chestnut eventer – an equine Rolls Royce who'd been well on the way to Advanced level before he'd developed navicular syndrome, the same problem Lightning had suffered from. His owner had been at the Pony Club area competition with her daughter, where there'd been a lot of talk among the parents about why Lightning wasn't shod, and soon afterwards she'd seen the article about the Hidden Horseshoe in the equestrian magazine. Having exhausted all other possibilities, she was keen to give the "barefoot treatment" a go. Chris and everyone at Newbridge Farm knew if they managed to cure Otto's lameness it would help the reputation of the Hidden Horseshoe Sanctuary tremendously.

The second horse to arrive was Humphrey the hunter, whose owner wanted him to have a rest during the summer. He was a weary-looking big bay horse with a Roman nose, a kind eye and dips behind his shoulders where his saddle hadn't fitted properly. If Otto was a Rolls Royce, Humphrey was a Land Rover Defender that had seen better days.

Bubble and Squeak, a couple of spotted Dartmoor hill ponies, had been bought by a pop star for his girlfriend as a Christmas present. They'd seen the scurry driving competition at Olympia, and fancied giving it a go. Unfortunately neither of them knew how to handle wild ponies so, after a few failed attempts, Bubble and Squeak had been turned away in a large, lush field, where they'd been perfectly happy until they'd developed laminitis from the spring grass.

Joe thought Bubble and Squeak looked like large

Dalmatians as they charged down the ramp of the impressive lorry that delivered them. It was difficult to see past the spots and imagine a normal pony underneath, somehow.

The driver handed their passports to Mum. "Never know what you're going to transport with this job. It was a top-class filly to Newmarket yesterday, and now I'm off to Scotland to pick up a couple of Clydesdales." He shook his head. "Don't think I've ever transported a Bubble and a Squeak before, though."

"Which one's which?" Joe asked.

"Bubble has more spots, apparently." He climbed into the lorry cab, shut the door and leant out of the window. "Happy counting!"

With several horses and ponies, all with different needs, and the grass becoming richer every day, the grazing had to be re-thought.

Horse safety was a priority at Newbridge Farm. Mum did everything by the book, and Joe reckoned she'd read all the books ever written on horses. They were always especially careful about introducing new horses to each other. The big barn made it easy, as strangers could get to know each other gradually.

After some initial squealing matches, Otto and

Humphrey got on well enough, so they were put in a field together.

ET and Lady had become firm friends so, although ET needed more food than Lady, they were kept together.

That left Lightning, Treacle, Bubble and Squeak, who all needed restricted grazing so they wouldn't get laminitis. Mum thought Lightning and Treacle would be a calming influence on Bubble and Squeak. The paddock behind the barn seemed the obvious place for them, as the grass was coarse and had recently been eaten down by some sheep from Lucketts Farm. It also had the advantage of being close to the stables.

They turned the ponies out together for the first time on a sunny Sunday morning. Joe and Emily led Lightning and Treacle, and Bubble and Squeak followed hesitantly, eyes bulging, snorting at everything. Mum walked behind quietly.

Once in the paddock, the ponies charged around a couple of times, chose places to roll and then settled down to graze – Lightning with Treacle and Bubble with Squeak. The sun shone through the leaves on some trees nearby, casting gentle dapples over everything.

Mum sighed happily. "Lovely," she said. "Okay, back to work. You two had better finish your homework and then get ready for the games practice this afternoon. Tracey said you should be at Lucketts by two o'clock if you want a lift. It'll be a sandwich lunch. We'll have a proper meal this evening, when Dad's back from playing golf."

At midday, Mum helped Emily and Joe bring the ponies back into the stables. "We'll put them out again tonight, and start the summer routine of out by night and in by day," she said. "The sooner the spotties can be led, the better. It's not easy with them skittering behind the other two."

"Treacle's turned into a spotty," Emily said as Mum walked away. "He's got old leaves and stuff all over him. I needn't have bothered to wash him this morning." She took off his head collar and fetched a grooming kit from the tack room. "Look! He's laughing. Cheeky monkey."

Joe peered through the bars separating the two stables. It really did look as if Treacle was laughing, with his head raised and his top lip curled up towards his nostrils. "Daft pony," he said, and turned his attention back to Lightning.

A few minutes later Emily said, "I think we woke him up; he keeps yawning. He must have gone to sleep in a damp patch . . . his tummy's all wet. I'm never going to get him clean in time . . . Ouch! Don't do that!"

"What's the matter?" Joe asked.

"Ow! He's done it again!" Emily wailed. "He tries to kick me when I brush his tummy. He's never, ever done that before. Ouch! See? No, Treacle!"

Joe heard a slapping noise, and looked up from buckling Lightning's girth. "Don't hit him!" he shouted. "What's got into you?"

Emily looked close to tears. "It's what's got into *him*, not me! He's like a completely different pony. I'll have to tie him up."

As she turned to get the head collar, Treacle's front legs crumpled, he sank to the stable floor with a groan and rolled vigorously, covering himself with sawdust. Afterwards he lay on his side, looked round at his tummy and yawned.

Emily started to cry. "What's wrong with him? Why is he being so *naughty*?"

A sickening feeling gripped Joe. "We'd better go and find Mum," he said. "Treacle isn't being naughty. He's ill. I think he may have colic."

Chapter 13

Their ordinary Sunday became horribly extraordinary.

Mum rang the vet, who said he'd come as quickly as possible. In the meantime they should try to keep the pony warm and comfortable. He suggested gentle exercise, as that often helped to relieve blockages or trapped air.

Emily was too upset to do anything, and she wanted to be with Mum, so Joe volunteered to go back to the stables.

Damp patches of sweat had appeared all over

Treacle's body, and his nostrils pulsated with rapid breaths. Joe brushed the sawdust off him as best he could and found a light rug. It had started to rain outside, so he led him up and down the central passage of the stable barn.

Lightning stretched her neck out in greeting every time Treacle passed by, but he took no notice. He walked hesitantly, swishing his tail, frequently stopping to kick at his stomach or try to sink down and roll.

"Hup! Hup! Walk on!" Joe urged, pulling at the lead rope. He tried to stay calm, but panic seeped in.

"How are you doing?"

Joe looked up to see Nellie standing in the passageway, her hair and clothes dripping. "Not too good. He seems to be getting worse."

"Your mum telephoned. Said you could use some company."

"Thanks." Joe smiled and felt his lips trembling.

She put a hand on his arm. "Okay?"

He nodded, not trusting himself to speak, and saw a blurry image of her smiling back. Thank goodness she'd come.

Nellie turned her attention to Treacle. "Let's have a look at you," she said, slipping her hand under his jaw bone. A look of intense concentration came over her and she moved her lips, as if counting silently. "Hm," she said. "Pulse about eighty."

"Is that bad?"

"Put it this way, a normal rate for a pony is around forty-five beats per minute." She gently lifted up Treacle's top lip and pressed his gums with her finger. "Hm," she said again, and put her head against Treacle's flank. Then she walked behind him and did the same on his other side.

"Haven't you got anything you can give him to make him better?" Joe asked. She knew so much about horses; surely she'd have some sort of cure.

"I think we'd better wait for the vet." Nellie looked worried. "Poor lad," she said, as if talking to herself. "Let him stand still, and I'll try to ease his pain a little." She faced Treacle, cupped her hands around his ears and began pulling them gently from base to tip. When she reached the tips she lingered, holding them between her thumb and forefinger. Then she pressed her fingers against Treacle's muzzle for a while before returning to his ears.

Gradually his head drooped, his body relaxed and his breathing became slower.

"It's working!" Joe exclaimed. "I knew you'd be able to cure him."

"This isn't a cure, I'm afraid. It's just making him more comfortable. You see, I'm using various pressure points to help him make his own painkillers. Here, you try."

Although Treacle was sweaty, his ears felt cold. Joe's shoulders and arms began to ache, but when he stopped the pony nudged him, begging him to continue.

After what seemed like ages, the vet arrived accompanied by Emily and Mum.

He put his stethoscope against various places on Treacle's body. Everyone stayed silent so he could listen. He packed the stethoscope away without saying a word, examined Treacle's gums and looked worried. Then he took Treacle's temperature by putting a thermometer up his bottom.

Poor Treacle, Joe thought, but he seemed past caring.

Emily giggled nervously.

Joe glared at her. Didn't she know that was the correct way to take a horse's temperature? She really could be incredibly immature sometimes.

Tracey and Caroline arrived as the vet was administering an injection. "I'm afraid this won't cure his colic, but it'll take away the pain for now," he said.

Caroline ran to her old pony and stroked his damp neck, then she hugged Emily. They both began to cry. Joe blinked furiously and stroked Treacle's ears.

"The signs aren't particularly promising, I'm afraid," the vet said, looking at Mum and Tracey in turn. "I'd like to have him back at the veterinary hospital, so we can observe him and operate if necessary, but it's entirely up to you. Is he insured?"

"Yes," said Mum.

The vet looked slightly happier. "Good. The sooner we can get this little chap to the surgery the better, then."

Tracey went to fetch the lorry.

"He will be okay, won't he?" Emily asked.

"We'll do everything we can for him, I promise you that," the vet said. He pulled his phone from his pocket. "I'll just ring ahead so they can get ready."

"I doubt whether you'll get a signal," Mum said. "Come into the house and use our phone."

They left Joe, Nellie, Caroline and Emily with Treacle.

Emily immediately burst into tears. "I t-thought h-he was b-being n-naughty," she stammered between sobs.

"Sshhh, Emily. You don't want to upset Treacle, do you?" Joe said quietly. "Come here, and I'll show you how to stroke his ears. It helps to take the pain away."

He showed Emily how to apply pressure as she slid her hands up Treacle's ears. She and Caroline took it in turns, pleased to be able to do something.

Treacle stood with his head down and a faraway expression on his face. It looked as if the vet's painkiller was doing its stuff. He didn't even stir when the horse lorry from Lucketts Farm pulled up outside with a hiss of brakes.

Chris got out of the cab. "Hi, I'm the ambulance driver," he said. "Tracey's stayed at home with Angus."

As if on auto-pilot, Treacle allowed himself to be half-led, half-carried up the ramp.

"Can I come with you?" Joe asked.

"Fine by me," Chris said. "Caroline, can you stay here with Emily?"

Caroline nodded. She seemed relieved.

As the lorry drove away, Joe caught sight of Emily and Caroline in the wing mirror, waving and calling out good-luck messages.

A smooth drive flanked by post-and-rail fencing led to the modern red-brick buildings of the veterinary hospital.

"Ever wondered why vets are so expensive?" Chris remarked with a wry smile as they drove in.

The vet was waiting for them. "Unload him straight into here," he said, pointing at a building with a large door, rather like a garage. The whole place smelled of disinfectant.

Groggy, shaky but completely trusting, Treacle followed Chris, step by step, down the ramp and into the sterile unit. Once there, the vet examined him again.

Joe hoped he'd say something encouraging, but the vet made no comment other than asking Chris to follow him to the office for a moment. They disappeared through an open side door, leaving Joe and Treacle alone together.

The little pony stood staring at nothing in particular, spaced out on painkillers. Images of a healthy, happy Treacle flashed through Joe's mind: galloping flat-out up the long field to Lucketts Farm with Chocolate Buttons by his side; wearing those ridiculous felt reindeer antlers on Christmas Day; patiently teaching Emily to ride; doing a lap of honour with Lightning and the rest of the team . . .

This didn't seem real, and yet it was. All too real.

They didn't talk much on the way home.

Chris flicked through some radio channels – frothy pop songs, sombre classical music, annoying chat shows, depressing news and finally silence, apart from the hum of the lorry.

"I'm afraid it doesn't look good," he said finally. "They think Treacle's got a twisted gut. They're operating immediately, but it's unlikely to be successful. If they can't do anything for him they won't bring him round from the operation, so at least he won't suffer."

"What caused it? Is it our fault?" The questions Joe had been aching to ask tumbled out.

"If it is a twisted gut, several things could have caused it but none of them will be anybody's fault," Chris said, turning his head briefly to give Joe a reassuring smile.

They lapsed into silence again. What else was there to say?

Joe thought about the horseshoe under his bed and his seven wishes. If only he'd kept some for later rather than making up silly ones which would never come true. He closed his eyes and wished anyway.

Chapter 14

Treacle never came round from the operation. His intestines were irreparable, so he was put to sleep there and then.

The vet said nobody was to blame. It was just really bad luck.

Unbelievable, unfair, devastating . . . No words could describe how Joe felt.

It was even worse for Emily. Her life had revolved around Treacle, and now he'd gone. Several times Joe found her crying helplessly over something that had triggered yet another memory: Treacle's hoof prints by the gate, his pink and purple turnout rug with dark brown hairs all over it in the tack room, or an open packet of his favourite pony treats on the shelf by the back door.

After a while she avoided the stables and fields altogether, preferring to stay in the house or walk up the road to Orchard Rise. A couple of Nellie's hens had hatched some chicks, and she spent hours with them.

Rusty became her constant companion. He even slept in her bedroom at night. Joe missed him, but he wasn't going to say anything. He knew that Emily's world had fallen apart; she needed all the comfort she could get.

Treacle and Emily were sorely missed by the Bellsham Vale mounted games team as well. It didn't help that the new team member, Lucy, appeared to think she was doing everyone a huge favour. In a way she was, because she was a good rider with a very good pony, but she created rifts in the team which hadn't been there before.

Lucy had done well at junior level, but had since chosen to concentrate on dressage and show jumping. However, she'd suddenly become keen on games again, so her parents had bought her an experienced

Prince Philip Cup pony – a sparky palomino called Bilbo.

"Some people have all the luck," Ali grumbled to Joe and Caroline in the school canteen one lunch time. "Just when I think I might get into the team at last, Lucy waltzes in with a fantastic pony. I love Ted to bits, of course, but Maria says he's too old for lots of fast work, so I'll have to carry on as reserve for this year." She brightened. "Did I tell you? I'm having Rolo next year! On loan from Maria, until her god-daughter can manage him."

"Wow! Lucky you!" Caroline exclaimed.

Ali looked gloomy again. "Trouble is, we won't have so much of a chance without Simon."

"Yes, I expect Lucy only decided to take up games again because he's in the team," Caroline said.

"Because he's a good rider, or because she fancies him?" Ali said with a mischievous grin.

"Both," Caroline said, grinning back.

The zone finals at the end of June didn't go according to plan. The standard was much higher than it had been at area level, and it took them by surprise.

Simon was even bossier than usual, but his chivvying only made things worse. The team was eliminated from the bending race because Minstrel charged over the line before Caroline had taken over the baton, and both Lucy and Sarah made mistakes in other races, mainly because they were vying for Simon's attention.

He became increasingly agitated as the scores stacked up. "We'll never get to HOYS at this rate," he kept saying. "It's okay for you guys, but I'm fifteen now; this is my last chance. *Come on!*"

They ended up coming third in the big sack race – a real test of team coordination – because Simon started jumping too fast and they all tumbled in a heap on top of him.

Over all, they came fifth out of seventeen, with twenty-two points. Now their only chance of qualifying for the Horse of the Year Show was to win the Pony Club Championships in the middle of August, where the final two spaces would be contested.

Defeat was their wake-up call. It made them see how hard they'd have to work if they wanted to do well. They'd have to pull together and work as a team, no matter what. That meant getting on with each other, making mounted games their number one priority and practising as much as possible. If they were to stand any chance of winning, they'd have to give it all they'd got.

*

Mum put all her energy into getting Emily another pony. She trawled the internet, horsey magazines and local newspapers in search of a replacement for Treacle. The kitchen table became littered with advertisements for ponies which were *sadly outgrown* or *for sale through no fault of their own*.

Emily barely glanced at them, but Joe studied each one, trying to read between the lines and guess what the pony was really like. He came to the conclusion that *to competitive home only* meant ridiculously expensive, *experienced* meant worn out, *potential to go to the top* meant unbroken and *stunning* meant lethal.

After some lengthy telephone conversations and email exchanges with their owners, Mum came to the same conclusion, but she pressed ahead anyway and compiled a shortlist of possible candidates.

"I've got some good news, Emily," she said one evening as they were eating supper. "Tracey and Caroline are both going to come and look at ponies with us next weekend. Isn't that kind of them?"

"Suppose so," Emily said awkwardly.

"You could be a little more enthusiastic, Pumpkin. Mummy's gone to a great deal of trouble," Dad said.

"Stop calling me Pumpkin! I'm not a baby anymore!" Emily exploded. "Go ahead and buy a pony if it makes you feel better, but don't expect me to ride it." She stormed upstairs to her room, slamming the door behind her.

"I only wanted to make things right," Mum said miserably.

Dad got up and gave her a hug. "I know, I know. Don't push it, though. Give her time."

The possibility that Emily might not want to have another pony made Joe surprisingly sad. The truth was that she'd helped him in all sorts of ways, from making friends at Pony Club to practising mounted games at home and looking after the horses. She'd even started to exercise Lightning for him sometimes, and he'd been glad they'd got on so well together because . . . Joe froze as an awful thought struck him.

What will happen to Lightning when I've grown out of her if Emily doesn't want her?

Chapter 15

J oe had the idea as he and Mum rode past Orchard Rise on Lightning and Lady, with Rusty following close behind.

One of Nellie's chickens had escaped into the road, and Rusty guided it back through the gate with all the style of the top-class sheepdog he'd been bred to be.

Joe felt a rush of pride. "Look at that! Isn't it amazing he's so good at rounding up chickens, yet he won't go anywhere near sheep?"

"Tracey told me he was really promising as a puppy, but a ewe with newborn lambs attacked him.

He's never forgotten it," Mum said. "Such a shame."

Joe smiled. "Not entirely. Caroline's dad wouldn't have given him to me otherwise, would he?"

"Very true."

"Mum?"

"Yes?"

"How about getting Emily some chickens?" Joe said.

"What a good idea," Mum replied. "The trouble is, I don't know the first thing about them, do you?"

"Not really," Joe admitted. "But Nellie does."

"Of course – the ideal person."

"I'll ask her, if you like."

"That would be great. Can we make it your project? We'll pay for whatever's needed, of course, but I've got a lot to do and Dad's fitting out the tack room at last, now the summer holidays have arrived."

Nellie was full of enthusiasm. "I've got some pullets you can have," she said. "That way Emily will have chickens she's known ever since they were day-old chicks. It'll make it more special for her."

"Oh, she'll love that. Thanks," Joe said.

"Where are you planning on keeping them? They'll need somewhere safe, so foxes and the like can't get in."

"They sell poultry arks at Landsdown Farmers, don't they?"

Nellie looked scornful. "Mm, I've seen them. Low-grade timber, cheap roofing felt, flimsy wire, and they don't even bother to use galvanised fixings. I'd save my money if I were you."

"We'll have to buy *something*, though." Joe paused. "Or—" Was this a silly idea? "Or I suppose we could make something. I mean, Dad's good at carpentry, and he's got lots of tools, so it wouldn't be impossible, would it?"

Nellie grinned, her weather-beaten face creasing into lots of little wrinkles. "Now you're talking! Let's make a chicken house to be proud of."

Over mugs of tea in the half-built tack room, Joe, Dad and Nellie designed a chicken house to be proud of. It had a high level sleeping area with perches at different levels, a window for light and air, a comfy nest box, a wide ladder leading down to a spacious vermin-proof run and wheels so it could be moved on to fresh grass every few days.

"This'll be a poultry palace!" Dad announced grandly.

Joe laughed, and wrote *Emily's Poultry Palace* at the top of their drawing. Then he rolled it up, secured it with a plaiting band and put it on the top shelf of an old bookcase they'd been using for temporary storage until proper cupboards and shelves had been made. As he did so, his hand knocked against something that shifted and clinked against something else. Joe felt along the shelf . . . two small horseshoes – old front shoes – unmistakably Treacle's.

"More rubbish?" Dad asked, without looking to see what Joe was holding. "Shove it on the pile over there. It's amazing how much junk has accumulated in just a few months. I'm going to have a trip to the dump when I've finished."

"No, it's okay. I'll keep these," Joe said, and hid them away in the pocket of his hoody.

Nellie must have seen what Joe had found, because she smiled and nodded her approval.

Dad said he'd take the mugs back to the house and phone the builders' merchants. If Emily saw everything being delivered tomorrow she'd think it was for the tack room, so that wouldn't be a problem, and their secret would be safe if they did all the construction in the stable barn.

Before he went to bed, Joe cleaned the dirt off Treacle's horseshoes and placed them carefully in the box under his bed. Then he sent Martin a message on Facebook, telling him about the poultry palace.

A reply came back almost immediately: *Count me in! I'll b round tomoz 2 help u build Cluckingham Palace!*
Trust Martin.

Chapter 16

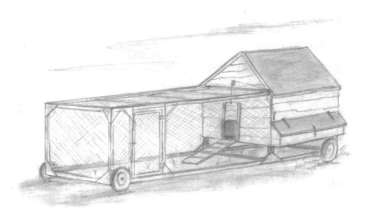

Martin arrived the following morning with a hammer and plenty of chicken jokes.

"Why did the chicken cross the road?"

"Everyone knows that," Joe replied. "To get to the other side."

"Okay. Why did the chicken cross the road, roll in mud and cross the road again?"

"Because he was a dirty double-crosser," Dad said.

"How did you know that?" Joe asked.

"A Christmas cracker in the pub," Dad replied. "Why do hens gossip?"

"Because talking is *cheep*," Nellie answered, surprising them. She put down a tray of tea and cake, surveying the chaos on the ground as she did so. "Haven't got very far, have you? Too many jokes and not enough action, eh?"

"Yes, we'll have to work around the cluck at this rate," Martin said.

They all groaned. Nellie handed them mugs of tea, and then the cake.

Chocolate cake – my favourite, Joe thought. It took all his willpower to pass on the plate without taking a piece.

Refusing food felt most peculiar, but there was a strict weight limit for riders in relation to the height of their ponies for mounted games, and over the past few months he'd grown so much taller that he was becoming far too close to Lightning's weight limit for comfort. If he wasn't careful he wouldn't be able to ride her in the zone finals or, if they got that far, the Horse of the Year Show. And he wanted to stay in the team even more than he wanted chocolate cake – most of the time, anyway.

Martin didn't help. "Sure you don't want any, Joe? It's delicious," he said, licking his fingers.

"Quite sure," Joe said quickly.

"You'd better have this bit, then," Nellie said to Martin. "Pity to waste it."

Joe's tummy rumbled. Lunch seemed a long way off.

Martin spent most of the following week at Newbridge Farm. He even stayed on to help Dad when Joe had to do other things, like looking after the horses with Nellie, exercising Lightning or going to games practice.

They made a good team, Joe thought. Perhaps the Pony Club games team should build a chicken shed together.

Maria's team-building events were ten-pin bowling in Bellsham or barbecues by the swimming pool at the Courtenays' house. They'd helped a lot, Joe had to admit. There was no more bickering and gossiping behind people's backs. They all looked out for each other now. The team had a family feel to it – a deep bond nobody could break even if petty differences surfaced every now and then.

After ten days Cluckingham Palace was almost ready. They carried each section out to a grassy area between the barn and the old orchard – where it couldn't be seen from the house – and assembled it there.

"Beautiful. A work of art," Dad said, standing back to admire it.

"I wouldn't mind living there," Martin said.

"In you go, then," Joe joked, pretending to push him through the door.

Nellie brought half a dozen point-of-lay pullets from Orchard Rise. They seemed to take to their new home instantly – what chicken wouldn't?

Joe felt a surge of satisfaction as they settled in, clucking and cooing at each other.

"Well done, everyone. A fantastic team effort," Dad said in a brisk, schoolmasterly voice. "Let's get everything tidied up. People will be arriving in half an hour."

Emily was helping Mum in the garden when Joe went to fetch her. Mum had been asked to keep her busy in a place where she wouldn't see preparations for the naming ceremony going on. By the look of relief on Mum's face, the task had been a challenging one.

"Come on, I've got a surprise for you," Joe said, trying to hide how excited he felt.

Emily looked at him suspiciously. "What kind of surprise?"

"A nice one, of course."

"Not a toad-in-the-hair sort of surprise?" She'd never forgiven him for that.

Joe smiled. "No, I promise."

Emily looked at Mum, who was wiping her hands on her gardening apron. "D'you know what it is, Mum?"

"Yes, I do. Don't worry, darling, you'll love it. Go on – go with Joe. I'm coming too, but he should be the first to show you because it was all his idea."

Joe held out his hand. Emily took it. Her hand was still gritty with earth. They walked past the house and up the path towards the stables. Rusty bounded ahead, eager to take charge of the hens once more. He either crouched down, eyeing them intently, or sprinted first one way and then the other around the run, making sure they were all gathered together.

At the entrance to the yard, Emily stopped. "The surprise isn't a new pony, is it?"

"No, it isn't. You said you didn't want a new pony – remember?"

They walked on. Emily hesitated again, but this time she was smiling. "It isn't Lightning, is it?"

"No, of course not. I've already told you it isn't a pony."

"You didn't! You said it wasn't a *new* pony."

Joe sighed. "Look, it isn't anything to do with ponies. Okay?"

Emily looked as if she was going to cry.

Oh goodness, this isn't going according to plan, Joe thought. "It's something to do with chickens," he whispered, to prevent any more upsetting guesses, "and there are some good friends around the corner, waiting for us, so please cheer up."

"Oh!" Emily exclaimed. She quickly washed her hands under the tap in the yard, rubbed her eyes, gave Joe a brave smile and took his hand again.

When she saw the poultry palace and her own special chickens, she couldn't control her tears, but at least they were tears of joy.

Caroline and her family, Martin and his parents and, of course, Nellie were guests at the Cluckingham Palace Presentation Ceremony. This was followed by a naming ceremony, and then each chicken had to be given a name as well. Eventually they went into the house for tea.

Later, as the Cox family was leaving, Joe asked Caroline to wait a minute. "I wasn't sure whether you'd want this or not, but then I thought you might, but if you don't I'll understand. It was Treacle's, you see," he mumbled, holding out one of the horseshoes he'd found in the tack room.

Caroline's hand brushed against his as she took it. "How did you know? I wanted to ask you if you had one, but then I didn't think I ought to, somehow.

Thanks so much, Joe." She hugged him, and he wrapped his arms around her in return.

He could feel the curve of her back beneath his hands. Her hair smelled freshly washed.

"Um, see you tomorrow at the games practice then," Caroline said.

"Er, yup. See you," Joe replied.

"Last one before the Championships."

"Don't remind me."

"Sorry, just have. Byee, see you!" She held the horseshoe up, grinned, then turned and sprinted after the others as they walked home up the hill.

Emily ran into the stable barn as Joe was grooming ET. "Guess what I've got!" She held out a pebble-like object. "My first egg!"

"Great. Shouldn't it be bigger than that, though?" Joe asked.

"Yes, I thought so too, but Nellie says pullets lay tiny eggs to begin with, then as they get more experienced they lay bigger and bigger eggs until they become grown-up hens and lay proper ones," Emily said.

"Ah, so hens are *egg*-sperienced, are they?" Joe asked.

Emily made a face at him. "You've been spending too much time with Martin."

Joe laughed. "Tell you what, put your precious egg somewhere safe in the tack room and come and help me brush the horses. You can do Lightning, if you like."

"Okay." Emily found a grooming kit in the tack room, and then went into Lightning's stable. "Hello, beautiful. Have you missed me? I've missed you *so much*," she said, giving her a hug.

Hurray for the chickens, Joe thought to himself. And that ridiculously tiny egg.

Chapter 17

The stately home looked magnificent in the evening sunlight as Chris drove the Lucketts Farm lorry into the crowded lorry park.

"Nice weather for camping," Caroline remarked.

"Yup, we could even have a swim in that lake over there," Joe said, trying to hide how awestruck he was by his surroundings. So this was where the Pony Club Championships were being held. What an amazing place!

Chris turned off the ignition, and the lorry fell silent. "The stables are over there, but don't put the ponies in straight away; lead them around for a while and let them nibble at some grass," he said. "I'll get the bedding and hay sorted."

So Joe and Caroline took Lightning and Minstrel for a walk. The ponies stepped out eagerly, taking in the sights, sounds and smells of the exciting place they'd been transported to. Joe wondered whether they appreciated their grand surroundings or were more concerned about the lush grass beneath their hooves and the horses and ponies passing by.

This wasn't just the mounted games championships, but the show jumping, dressage, polocrosse and cross-country championships as well. Horses, ponies and people were everywhere. Several riders smiled and said hello as they came within talking distance.

A tall, slim boy riding an elegant grey pony approached them. "Hi, are you here for the mounted games?" he asked in a Scottish accent.

"Yup, that's right," Joe said.

"What team are you?"

"Bellsham Vale," said Joe. "You?"

"I'm Angus."

"My brother's called Angus, too," Caroline said.

The boy laughed. "Sorry, I meant I belong to the Angus Pony Club. My name's Harry. Harry Fraser."

"Oh, I see! I'm Caroline and this is Joe. Your pony's

beautiful. I love dappled greys. What breed is she?" Caroline held her hand out for the pony to sniff, then stroked her nose gently.

"Fortune's mostly thoroughbred, with a bit of Connemara thrown in to make her sensible," Harry said. "A pony in a million, but I'll have to give her back after this year. She's only on loan, you see, and I'm getting too tall for her. Besides, I'll be too old for the Prince Philip Cup next year."

"I'm getting too tall for Lightning as well," said Joe. "I'd love to carry on next year though, if we can afford to get a bigger pony without selling this one."

Harry looked astonished. "What's your pony called again?"

"Lightning," Joe said, stroking her neck.

"I can't believe it!" Harry jumped off Fortune and hurried towards Lightning. "How amazing! It really is you, isn't it?" he said, making a big fuss of her.

Joe stared at him, speechless.

"She used to be ours," Harry explained, his eyes bright with emotion. "My brother Robbie rode her. They were brilliant together – in the Prince Philip Cup finals two years running, and they did well jumping too. Strathearn was our Pony Club then."

Of course! Joe thought. "Auchterarder," he said out loud. "Is that how you pronounce it?"

Harry looked taken aback. "Near enough," he

replied. "How do you know where we used to live?"

"The address was in the passport. I wrote to someone called Moira Fraser because I wanted to find out about Lightning."

"Moira Fraser's my mum. But we moved from Auchterarder about four years ago, when my parents split up."

"That explains why she never replied to my letter," Joe said.

"The worst part was that we had to sell the ponies," Harry went on. "Mine went to friends, so that was kind of okay, but we sold Lightning to some people who wanted her for a Pony Club team somewhere down south. They promised to give us first refusal if they decided to sell her, but we never heard from them again. We were told they'd moved abroad and she'd been sold, but nobody seemed to know what had happened to her. It was really bad."

No wonder I didn't get a reply from the other letter either, Joe thought.

A tall, slim lady wearing sunglasses came up to them.

"Guess who I've found, Mum," Harry said, beaming at her.

"It can't be!" she exclaimed as she rushed to Lightning's side. "Oh my goodness, it is!" She stroked her all over in a kind of trance, saying things like, "It really is you," and, "You're looking wonderful, my pet," and, "Well I never, Robbie's Lightning pony!"

Lightning bent her head round, her eyes soft and content.

She remembers, Joe thought. She loves these people too. He felt an odd mixture of happiness, curiosity and jealousy. It was great to find out something about her past, and to solve the mystery of why she was so good at games, yet it was strange to think she'd belonged to another boy and they'd been "brilliant together".

Harry's mum gave Joe a big smile. "It's wonderful to see how well Lightning is. I was so worried about her, not knowing where she might have ended up. I must phone Robbie and tell him. He'll be over the moon!"

Joe smiled back. He had the same feeling about Harry and his mum that he'd had about Caroline and Chris when he'd first met them: they'd be good friends.

The mounted games competition in the morning was for teams that hadn't qualified previously for the Horse of the Year Show, and the one in the afternoon was for teams that had. Only the two winners – one in the morning and one in the afternoon – would get to the Horse of the Year Show, so there was no room for mistakes.

Joe and Caroline watched Harry compete in the morning. He and Fortune were great together, as Joe had guessed they would be. They covered the ground fluently, changing direction and speed through communication so subtle it seemed invisible.

Joe remembered something Nellie had said about riding: "If it looks beautiful and effortless, you've got it right."

Harry had definitely got it right. Joe had never wanted to do mounted games on any pony other than Lightning, but as he watched he found himself wondering how it would feel to ride Fortune . . .

The Angus team deserved to win their competition and they did, with several points to spare. They'd be going to the Horse of the Year Show, lucky things!

Joe felt he had to do well more than ever now. Harry and his mum would be watching. He wanted them to see that he and Lightning could be brilliant together too . . . He wanted to do his best for the team . . . He wanted to *win*.

His body felt super-charged with nerves as the ponies and riders for the afternoon competition gathered in the collecting ring. This was it! Winner takes it all. He looked down at his hands. They were shaking.

Caroline rode up beside him. "Osu!" she said, smiling.

His eyes met hers, and he smiled back. "Osu!"

Lessons learned in aikido came back to him all of a sudden: the need for a calm, clear mind; the importance of feel, focus, timing and balance.

"Be quick, but don't hurry," Sensei Radford had said. "In other words, you need to operate with speed *and* precision."

Joe closed his eyes for a moment and concentrated hard on becoming calm and focused. Speed and precision, speed and precision, he told himself. I will do my absolute best, no matter what . . .

A few races into the competition, Joe realised he was enjoying every moment. The pressure of having to win didn't worry him any more – in fact, it was exciting. The other teams were good, but the Bellsham Vale appeared to be even better. All those hours of preparation and training made sense now. Everything had clicked into place. At last Joe felt that his riding was matching Lightning's skill. He wasn't her passenger, he was her partner. He could feel truly proud to be a member of the team, without any doubt that he'd been chosen because of his pony.

Life doesn't get more perfect than this, Joe thought as he and the others lined up to receive their first rosettes. The majestic parkland seemed almost too beautiful to belong in the real world, the weather was ideal – warm and sunny with the hint of a breeze – and he could see Harry and his mum standing at the ringside, clapping and smiling. He stroked Lightning and told her what a good girl she'd been, even though he had a feeling she knew already.

Soon they were cantering, five abreast, in a lap of honour round the arena. Next stop Birmingham, the National Exhibition Centre and the Horse of the Year Show! A few hours ago it had seemed almost impossible. Now it felt as if they could achieve anything – even winning the Prince Philip Cup.

Chapter 18

A couple of days after the championships, Joe got a friend request on Facebook from Harry Fraser. He accepted it straight away, and took a look at Harry's page. His profile picture was of him racing through bending poles on Fortune, with a huge house that looked like a castle in the foreground and blue-tinged mountains in the background. The general effect was amazing, but what really caught Joe's eye was that Harry was riding without a saddle or bridle.

Joe sent him a message immediately: *Hi, Harry.*

Cool profile pic! Hope you & Fortune are OK. Lightning is fine. Can't believe we're going to HOYS!!!

In no time at all there was a reply: *Can't get my head round it either – bring it on! Back to school tomorrow. What about you?*

Joe replied: *We've got nearly two weeks left. Why so early?*

Harry wrote: *We work harder in Scotland! Autumn term v. long but 2 wks half term. Got to go into town now – shopping for shoes and trousers. Grown AGAIN!*

Know the feeling, Joe replied. *Having to watch what I eat till HOYS. Not fun. Miss chips and crisps most.*

That evening Harry wrote again: *Chocolate and bacon butties for me!*

From then on, Joe and Harry often made contact on Facebook. Joe sent photos of Lightning and the other horses at Newbridge Farm, and Harry sent lots of photos of Fortune competing in mounted games, show jumping, dressage and cross-country; she seemed to be good at all of them. There were also photos of her galloping along a sandy beach and playing in the snow with a couple of Shetland ponies called Douglas and Hamish.

Joe made the most of the rest of the holidays. He went fishing with Martin, rode with Caroline, took Rusty for long walks and accompanied Chris on his farriery rounds. Everything about farriery and horseshoes fascinated Joe. He loved watching Chris work, and it was interesting going to different places and meeting horses and their owners.

Fired up by their success and the prospect of competing at the Horse of the Year Show, the mounted games team threw themselves into an intensive training programme which involved regular mounted games practices, an exercise plan for the ponies and fitness sessions in Bellsham Leisure Centre for the riders.

As well as games techniques, they practised everything Maria could think of, from coping with loud noises and bright lights to rehearsing their lap of honour in case they won.

Joe had never been so fit in his life. He was almost bursting with energy, which was just as well because he had to cram a huge amount into every day. He got up early and took Rusty for a run before school, then rode Lightning on his return before doing his homework.

One day, as he went to find Lightning in her stable after school, he heard Emily chatting away to someone. He fully expected to find Mum or Nellie in the stable barn with her, but there was nobody to be seen. All he could hear was Emily talking . . .

He found her sitting on Lightning's back. Lightning had lots of little plaits in her mane; her ears pricked forwards as she noticed Joe and her nostrils fluttered in silent greeting, but Emily didn't notice.

". . . so I don't know whether Keely still wants to be best friends or not, because Vicky says . . ."

Joe felt he was intruding, so he tiptoed away. He'd do some homework and come back later. He didn't want to do anything to upset Emily or discourage her from becoming fond of Lightning again.

When he returned an hour later, Emily had vanished and Lightning had a slightly crinkly mane where her plaits had been.

In the final few days leading up to the Horse of the Year Show, Joe didn't see Emily in the stables again, but Lightning often had a crinkly mane and tail.

Only two days left! Joe thought as he helped Mum pack up all the things they'd need to take to the Horse of the Year Show.

"Joe? There's something I want to ask you," Mum said.

When Mum said something like that it was usually the start of a fairly serious conversation. Joe's heart sank. "What?" he said unenthusiastically.

"Do you think you'll want to carry on with Pony Club after this year?"

He hadn't expected that question, although secretly he'd been thinking about it a lot. "Er, I don't know, really," he said. "I mean, it's such a shame I'm growing out of Lightning; she'll be a tough act to follow."

Mum's face showed she had something tricky to say and wasn't sure how to go about it. "Yes, I know," she said. "Good games ponies are worth their weight in gold – almost literally." She took a deep breath. "You see, I've been approached by the Waterfields."

"Who?"

"You know, darling – Jess' parents. Jess Waterfield's in the Pony Club with you. She's got a strawberry roan pony called Poppy?"

"Oh yes," Joe said, remembering the girl who'd been on the leading rein at the Christmas rally. Her father had been very competitive, and they'd been amazingly quick. He'd seen Jess a few times since as well – doing mounted games off the leading rein – she'd become a pretty good rider actually. "Isn't she in the junior mounted games team?" he asked.

Mum smiled. "Yes, that's right. You see, Poppy's not fast enough now that Jess is off the leading rein and wanting to compete, so her parents have asked me if we'd consider selling them Lightning."

Joe stared at her.

"They've offered an incredible amount of money for her," she said. "And Dad and I were thinking that if we sold her to them we'd have enough money to buy you a really good pony so you can carry on riding."

Joe still couldn't bring himself to say anything. He'd been expecting things to come to a head some time in the future, but not like this. Not now, when he was so excited about HOYS.

"Lightning will have a caring, knowledgeable home with the Waterfields. Jess is the eldest of four, so it'll be a long-term home as well."

Joe broke his silence. "What if it isn't? What if they sell her on?"

"We could ask them to promise us first refusal."

"That's what the people who bought her from Harry's mum promised, but it didn't mean a thing."

"This is different. We'd be selling to local people we know. We can keep an eye on her."

"What about Emily? She loves her, you know."

Mum sighed. "We all love Lightning, darling. However, as Emily appears to have no intention of riding again, there's not much point in keeping a pony for her. Lightning will be wasted here stuck in a field with nothing to do. You often say how much she enjoys being ridden and competing, don't you?"

"If Lightning's here, I'm sure Emily will start riding her. She just needs time." Joe said.

"Oh dear," Mum said. "Let's leave this until after HOYS, shall we? We'll discuss it properly then, but the reality is that we won't be able to keep Lightning and buy you another top-class pony so you can carry on competing – we simply haven't got that sort of money."

"Then there's nothing to discuss," Joe said. "We'll keep Lightning."

That evening, Joe messaged Harry about his decision.

Harry replied straight back: *Sorry to hear that, but total respect. She's a lucky pony. If this'll be the first and last PPC for both of us, we'd better make it one to remember!*

Chapter 19

Shirley . . . Solihull . . . Signs to familiar places around Birmingham flicked by, but they weren't important to Joe now. The only signs they needed, as they trundled down the motorway in the Lucketts Farm lorry, were to the NEC and then, as they got nearer, to the Horse of the Year Show lorry park.

What would Lightning think of it all? Joe wondered. This morning she'd been in a grassy field with her friends. Now she'd been transported into this industrial, alien landscape with hardly a blade of grass in sight. How could she possibly feel at ease in such a place?

His fears were unfounded. She walked confidently with him through the overcrowded lorry park to the temporary stable blocks beyond, looking totally at home. Perhaps she'd known that all the frantic practising and preparations of the past few weeks were leading to this.

The stable blocks were in chaos, with everyone staking their claim and sorting out who and what went where. Parents and helpers were trying to create their team tack rooms, install hanging baskets of flowers and put nameplates on stable doors. The stable management competition was taken almost as seriously as the Prince Philip Cup itself.

Dad had made the Bellsham Vale tack room in pre-fabricated sections, and he'd taken the day off work to construct it on site.

Chris had put his blacksmithing skills to good use making the nameplates for the stable doors. Each pony's name had been fashioned from a long, thin strip of iron on a polished wooden plinth: Lightning, Minstrel and Rolo on one side with Flicka and Bilbo opposite. The tack room was in the sixth stable. If there were marks for craftsmanship, Joe thought, the Bellsham Vale would come top.

Almost all the competitors and their parents knew each other by now, and there was a lot of talk, teasing and good-natured rivalry.

"Hello, my Facebook friend!" a distinctly Scottish voice said as Joe was hanging up Lightning's haynet.

"Harry! How are you doing? Good to see you!"

They shook hands over the stable door. It was odd seeing Harry in person again – a little awkward, even – having developed such a close friendship online.

"Aye, we'll probably be sick of the sight of each other by Sunday. I'm your next-door neighbour here."

"Great! I hoped you would be when I saw the Angus was next to us."

Harry grinned. "I'll see you later when I've settled in Fortune. Mind you, she's such a pro she's taking it all in her stride. It's me who needs settling in."

Joe smiled. "Ditto."

By the evening everything had been sorted out, from tack rooms to team sweatshirts – yellow for the Bellsham Vale.

Their tack room was a masterpiece, with lovely finishing touches like framed display boards for every pony. Each had an old horseshoe, painted silver, on top. Lightning's board had a horseshoe on top as well, but not one she'd ever worn. It had been Joe's idea to put Treacle's shoe up there, and to devote the top part of the board to him. After all, he'd been a part of the team; he'd helped them win the area competition.

*

Joe lay awake throughout the first night. His camp bed in the back of the lorry was narrow and creaked whenever he moved, he couldn't block out the traffic noise from the nearby motorway, rain hammered down on the roof and images spiralled around in his head. He thought about the competition, but it made him jittery. He wondered if Lightning was asleep in her stable or wide awake like him . . . Thinking about her set him off worrying about her future. What would she want, if she could choose? Was he being stupid and selfish, wanting to keep her rather than letting the Waterfields have her? She'd have a good home there, he knew that, but even so they might not take care of her feet properly; it was a complicated business, and you had to be really careful about giving her a balanced diet with all the right minerals and stuff . . . No, Newbridge Farm was her home. He couldn't imagine her anywhere else. Selling Lightning would be like selling Rusty – unthinkable. He wondered what it was like to be a pony – passed from one place to the next as children grew out of you and discarded you like an old pair of shoes. Different owners, strange horses, unfamiliar ways . . . And what about Fortune? Who had her owner got lined up for her? Joe hoped it was someone like Harry – someone who'd deserve her . . .

Each day started at five in the morning, when they had to go for a practice in the arena. Breakfast followed at seven, and then a rest until eleven o'clock. Some people got a couple of hours' sleep, but Joe found he couldn't. By then the NEC was open for the day and there was too much noise. Lunch was at midday, and afterwards they had to get the ponies ready for the afternoon performance. After that there was tea at five o'clock, a little while off and then it was time for the evening performance. They finally went to bed at about eleven o'clock. It was surprising how quickly they all became used to this strange routine.

They rode in their teams to and from the actual competitions in the main arena, but the early morning practice sessions were much more relaxed, and Joe and Harry waited for each other so they could ride together.

On the second morning, as they were about to set off back to the stables, Harry jumped off Fortune and held her reins out to Joe. "Let's swap. Don't worry – I know I'm too big for Lightning. I'll lead her. The walk will do me good."

"Are you sure?" Joe asked.

"Sure I'm sure."

Joe dismounted, they swapped ponies, and he vaulted onto Fortune. She was nearly a hand taller than Lightning, and his leg only just cleared the back of her saddle.

The saddle was larger all round and its contours were unfamiliar. Even when he stretched his legs, his toes didn't make contact with the stirrup irons – like a little kid having a pony ride. Joe decided not to waste time adjusting leathers; instead, he crossed them over.

Her colouring and size were different, of course, but in many ways Fortune was so similar to Lightning that Joe felt completely at home on her.

"Okay?" Harry asked.

"Yup, fine." Joe grinned at him.

"To the stables, then. I need food, and lots of it."

Fortune didn't have to walk many strides for Joe to tell he was riding no ordinary pony. It felt more like floating on a cloud than walking. She was so light and responsive that he just had to think what he wanted to do and she did it immediately. He experimented several times: *right a bit, left a bit, faster, slower* . . . She cooperated willingly.

Harry laughed as he walked along with Lightning by his side. "Stop testing her, Joe. Didn't you believe me when I told you she's a pony in a million?"

"Of course I did. I know how well she goes for you, but I didn't dare hope she'd be so good with me as well. She's – she's gorgeous," Joe said.

After that, Harry let Joe ride Fortune every day, and every day Joe loved her even more.

He wished he had the courage to ask Harry whether he could contact Fortune's owner in case there was any chance of having her on loan. But at the same time he felt guilty about wanting another pony when he still had Lightning. It seemed so disloyal, when her only fault was that she'd stopped growing and he hadn't. If only Emily wanted to ride her!

As the days went by, the goal posts moved for the Bellsham Vale team. Riding in the Prince Philip Cup was no longer enough; they were out to win it.

Gradually nothing else mattered to Joe. Even his worries about Lightning and Fortune faded into the background. Soon he'd be able to eat normally, sleep normally, live normally and worry about normal things. But for now his world was the competition – one moment picking up tiny pieces of sawdust outside Lightning's stable and dusting off his grooming kit so the team would get good marks for stable management, and the next pushing his riding skills further than he thought possible under the glare of hot spotlights, watched by a cheering crowd and millions of television viewers all over the world.

Life didn't get much more surreal, and yet it had never felt more real.

Chapter 20

Before long it was Sunday; the last day of the show; the day of the Prince Philip Cup final.

First they had to qualify in the afternoon competition, because only four out of the six teams could go forward to the final in the evening.

The Angus had won the Equimax Cup on Thursday afternoon, but since then the Oakley had led for most of the way, with the Angus and the Bellsham Vale in hot pursuit. The tension for the riders had become relentless, whereas for the spectators it was a passing entertainment.

Dad and Emily arrived in the middle of the morning. They'd left Nellie holding the fort at home. Joe met them and took them to get stable passes because Mum was helping to cook lunch in the canteen. Emily skipped along.

Nice to have that sort of energy, Joe thought. His eyes ached and his skin felt prickly-tired, but he was fuelled by the knowledge that this was the final day – the day they'd all worked for, the day when they could win the Cup if they pulled out all the stops.

"How's the tack room?" Dad asked.

"Great," Joe replied. "The judges loved it and the other teams hate us. You wouldn't believe how seriously the parents are taking the stable management cup. Some of the teams even have leaf-blowers for cleaning the passageway outside the stables."

Emily's eyes were wide with indignation. "Isn't that cheating?"

"Apparently not. Mum said she would have brought her vacuum cleaner if she'd known."

They all laughed.

"I can't wait to see Lightning. How is she?" Emily asked.

"Weary, like me."

Emily and Joe stopped by Lightning's stable while Dad went on to admire the tack room.

She was lying down, dozing. When she saw Emily

and Joe, her nostrils flickered but she made no attempt to stand. Emily wanted to go in with her, but Joe said she needed all the rest she could get. They'd come back later.

They joined Dad in the tack room. He was examining the finer points of the joinery, but Emily's attention was immediately grabbed by the photos of Treacle.

She traced the outline of his shoe with her finger. "Oh," she said quietly. "I didn't realise you'd done that."

"No, I know. I'm sorry I didn't tell you. I didn't want to upset you all over again. But I thought Treacle deserved to be up there – and you," Joe said.

"Thanks," Emily said, and tears started to trickle down her face.

Dad swept her into his arms. "Let's go and find Mum, shall we?"

On the way to the lorry park, they passed Harry deep in conversation with a tall, grey-haired lady dressed in a smart tweed suit. Joe raised his hand in greeting, but Harry was too engrossed to notice.

"Do you know that lady?" Dad asked.

"No. Why?" Joe replied.

"She came to the farm yesterday. Said she wanted to take a look because she's thinking of sending a horse to us."

"What sort of horse?" Joe asked.

"I haven't a clue. Nellie showed her round."

"How odd that Harry knows her," Joe said.

They met Chris near the lorry park, and Dad stopped for a chat. Then Tracey came up with Sarah's mum, and before long everyone was deep in conversation. Joe's eyes closed, the chatter passed by him and he drifted away . . . He came to with a start.

"Have you been asleep on your feet? I said have you seen Emily?" Dad asked in a slow, deliberate voice.

"Uh? No, sorry. Should I have done?" Joe asked blearily.

"She must have wandered off while we were talking. If you go back to the stables, I'll see if she's gone to find Mum."

Joe thought Emily would be in the tack room, but she wasn't. She was in Lightning's stable, sitting in the sawdust beside her as she lay dozing.

"There you are! We were worried you were lost," he said as he entered the stable.

"Well, I'm not. I'm just giving Lightning a pep talk."

"A pep talk!"

"Yes, I was telling her I'll love her forever and so will Treacle. He'll be watching – I know he will – and he'll be with her all the way, especially when she does that lap of honour at the end, like we did at the area competition. That was such fun, wasn't it? The best day of my life," said Emily. She smoothed Lightning's mane over, gently picking out little bits of sawdust. "Lightning started it, didn't she? She helped us all to become friends."

Now Joe felt close to tears. "Yes, she did," he said.

"You know when you gave me the chickens?" Emily said.

Joe nodded his head, wondering what on earth that had to do with anything.

"I thought, well actually I *hoped*, the surprise would be Lightning. She's the only pony I've ever really wanted – apart from Treacle, of course."

Joe stared at her. "Why didn't you say anything?"

"'Cos of what you said that time."

"When?" Joe asked.

"On my birthday."

"I don't remember," Joe said, puzzled.

Emily sniffed loudly. "You said, 'Emily may have Treacle, but Lightning's mine. Nothing will ever change that.'"

"I didn't!" Joe protested.

"You did!" Emily exclaimed. "I thought I'd upset you somehow, so I followed you to the stables. You knew I was there and you said it loud and clear, so I'd hear!"

There was a stunned silence. Eventually Joe said, "I swear I didn't realise you were there, Emily. I was angry, that's all. I wanted to be a member of the Pony Club too." It sounded so stupid, so petty – so long ago. "The truth is, I want you to have her more than anything." He stroked Lightning. "And I hope you'll come to the Horse of the Year Show with her – it's the greatest fun."

Emily jumped up and gave Joe a hug. She grinned up at him, her old cheeky self. "I wonder what it's like to win the Prince Philip Cup."

"Stick around, and with any luck I'll be able to tell you," Joe said.

Chapter 21

Lightning craned her head over her door to sniff Fortune as Harry led her back into the stable next door.

"You're going to miss your friend when we go home tomorrow, aren't you?" Joe said.

"Perhaps not," Harry replied, turning so the two ponies could greet each other properly.

"I bet she will," Joe said. "Look at them."

Harry smiled, watching as they put their heads side-by-side, sharing a secret conversation. "Discussing tactics," he said.

"We'll need all the tactics we can get," Joe said. "That was far too close for comfort – only two points in it."

"At least both our teams will be riding this evening. That's the main thing."

"Suppose so," Joe said. "But we'll have some catching up to do."

"Double points in the final, remember. Anything could happen."

"Trouble is, it's usually the unexpected that *does* happen, isn't it? Fancy coming last in the bending! We almost always win that. Poor Caroline was so upset. She hardly ever knocks poles over."

"Combination of bad luck and nerves, I expect," Harry said.

"Yes, I think the pressure's getting to everyone now," Joe replied.

Harry's mum came into view, walking towards them, talking animatedly to the smart lady dressed in tweed.

"You haven't met Mrs McCulloch yet, have you?" Harry asked.

Joe shook his head. "Nope, but Dad said she went to our farm yesterday. Apparently she's got a horse she wants us to look after."

Harry laughed. "You still haven't guessed?"

Joe shook his head. "Guessed what?" he asked,

but Harry had turned to greet the visitors.

"Hello, Joe. We've never met, but I've heard a great deal about you. I was so delighted when Moira told me that Lightning was in good hands – she's such a special pony." The smart lady stroked Lightning, and then Fortune. "They get on famously, don't they? I'm Sandra McCulloch, by the way. Fortune's owner."

"Oh! Hello," Joe said. So this was Fortune's owner! The person he'd longed to meet. The person he'd longed to ask . . .

"Harry suggested that you may be able to give Fortune a good home. Do you think that might be possible?"

Joe realised he must have fallen asleep on his feet again. He didn't want to wake up from this dream, though – not just yet. It was too good!

"She's eighteen, so she's getting on a bit, but she should be fine for a few more years, and she does so love mounted games."

Joe tried to wake himself up, but everyone was still there and Sandra McCulloch was saying, "I've just talked to your parents about having Fortune, and they seem keen on the idea. But it's entirely up to you."

"Yes, please," he said. "I mean, thank you very much. I'd love to ride Fortune." Oh dear, that sounded as if he just wanted to make use of her. "And look after her," he added quickly. "I'll try my best to take good care of her, I promise."

Sandra McCulloch held Joe with her steady, smiling eyes. "I know you will. That's why I've asked you." She shook Joe's hand firmly. "Lovely to meet you at long last, Joe. I'd better go and find your parents again. Good luck this evening, in case I don't see you before then. And good luck to you as well, Harry."

As she walked away with Harry's mum, Joe said, "Tell me I haven't imagined this."

Harry laughed. "Okay. You haven't imagined this."

As if to confirm the fact, Joe's mobile phone started to vibrate in his pocket. He answered it.

"Hello? Is that you, Joe?"

"Oh. Hi, Martin."

"Did you get through to the final?"

"Yes. Just."

"Hurray! They got through to the final, everyone!" Martin shouted. There was a sound of cheering in the background.

"Where are you? In the pub?" Joe asked.

"No, you idiot! We're here, outside the NEC: Dad, Mum, Nellie, Sensei Radford, Darren, Spike, Andrew, Jack . . . A whole bunch of us. Dad hired a minibus and we've come along for the grand finale!" Another cheer from the background.

"You're mad, d'you know that?" Joe said, laughing.

"Can we meet up?" Martin said.

"Not for long, but I'll see you outside the main entrance in ten minutes if you like."

"Ideal."

Joe made sure Lightning had fresh water and a full haynet, and went to find Martin.

Crowds were already making their way to the main entrance, eager to fit in some shopping before the evening performance. An elderly couple were among them. They looked strangely familiar, even from the back.

Joe studied them more closely. Yes, it *was*! "Granny! Grandpa!" he called.

They looked round and waved enthusiastically, beaming with pleasure.

He reached Granny first, and gave her a big hug The smell of her perfume brought back so many memories.

"What are you doing here?" Joe asked.

"What do you think?" Grandpa replied, ruffling Joe's hair like he always used to. "We couldn't miss you winning the final now, could we? Especially as we live so near."

Being reminded of the final made Joe's stomach contract and his palms prickle with sweat. He attempted a smile. "No pressure, then?" he joked.

Gran squeezed Joe's hand. "Take no notice, my darling. Win or lose, we couldn't be more proud. You just go and do your best, and we'll be there cheering you on."

Simon gathered his team around before they mounted for the final. "This is the moment we've all worked so hard for," he said. "We can't afford any mistakes this time." He looked straight at Caroline.

She blushed and mumbled, "Sorry."

Everyone looked uncomfortable.

Joe glowered at him.

He avoided Joe's stare. "Okay, let's go! Good luck, everyone!"

Joe put his hand on Caroline's shoulder as they rode along. "Don't worry about Simon. Just focus on the game and do your best. Nothing else matters. Osu! Remember?"

She gave him a trembling smile. "Thanks, Joe. Osu!"

"And now, ladies and gentlemen, the moment you've all been waiting for: the Prince Philip Cup Final!"

Joe could hear the applause from the arena. The ponies jigged on the spot. Some tried to plunge forward, unable to contain their excitement a moment longer. He felt the hairs on the nape of his neck standing up. The curtain went back and they galloped side-by-side into the noise and glaring lights. This was it!

The commentator's voice rose over the noise from the crowd: "The first Prince Philip Cup competition was held at the Horse of the Year Show in 1957, and it has been a popular feature ever since. It was devised by His Royal Highness The Duke of Edinburgh to produce a spectacular competition that would test the skills and teamwork of, as he put it, 'ordinary children on ordinary ponies'. The selection process started in the spring, when over two hundred and fifty rival Pony Club teams competed against each other in one of nineteen Pony Club areas. After that there were the zone finals in June. The winners at each of the four zone finals qualified automatically for the Horse of the Year Show, and the final two places were contested at the Pony Club Championships in August. These six teams have been battling it out all week, first for the Equimax Cup and then, since Thursday evening, for the Prince Philip Cup. The four teams before you now are the finalists, so please give a warm welcome to the Angus!"

Applause, together with a few cheers, echoed around the arena.

"The Bellsham Vale!"

Joe still couldn't get used to hearing the name over the loudspeaker; it took him by surprise every time. Was he imagining it, or was the clapping louder? That was definitely Martin's piercing whistle.

"The Devon and Somerset!"

More applause.

"And finally, the current leaders, the Oakley Hunt West!"

Even more applause.

"But there's still everything to play for this evening, with double points on offer. Yes, I'll repeat that: double points! That means eight points for first place, six for second, four for third and two for fourth. And now for the first race – bending. Remember, ladies and gentlemen, the louder you cheer the faster they'll go!"

There were seven races in all. To begin with, the Bellsham Vale did really well: first in the bending – their speciality – and second in the ball and cone.

The stepping stone race came next. It was still the one Joe worried about most, even though he'd done well in it all week.

Breathe, focus, concentrate – and – go! Lightning surged forward. Joe did a flying dismount without slowing her down, ran for all he was worth to the stepping stones, crossed them with speed and precision, matched his stride with Lightning's and swung himself into the saddle again. She flattened out and galloped over the line as his hand touched Simon's. It was only then that Joe realised they were in the lead.

Simon's feet seemed to barely touch the ground, he ran so fast.

The team waited anxiously for the results to go up. Even when you thought you'd won, sometimes you hadn't because of a mistake spotted by the judges . . . Yes! They'd won!

They started the parcel race in high spirits, all thinking the same thing: *keep this up, and we could win the Cup!*

Caroline went first, then Lucy, then Joe. Lightning held steady as he placed his parcel on top of the two larger ones, and she raced back to the line as soon as he signalled it was okay to go. Sarah, too, balanced her smaller carton exactly on top, and handed over to Simon, the last to ride, with a lead of nearly half the length of the arena. They were on course to win again!

Rolo charged down to the far end of the arena, Simon swooped down, picked up the tiniest carton from the floor and urged Rolo on towards the stack in the middle. The crowd started to clap and cheer with delight as Rolo gathered himself up into a sliding stop by the parcels. Simon reached out to place the last one on top, but Rolo had been going too fast and he hadn't come to a halt yet. The tiny cube overbalanced and toppled to the ground.

"Oooh!" the crowd went.

Simon turned Rolo too sharply as he jumped off to retrieve the cube and the whole stack came tumbling down.

Joe and the others watched helplessly, in shock. Simon and Rolo were the best – they never made mistakes!

Simon worked quickly. He'd just about balanced the stack when the other ponies galloped by, upsetting Rolo who barged into it again, scattering the parcels even further.

The commentator made jokes and the crowd loved it; they roared with laughter as the scene became like a slapstick comedy. Simon persevered, finally managed to rebuild the stack and crossed the finish line last, to clapping and whistles from the audience.

"We can still do it!" he said desperately as they all gathered around him after the scores were announced. "It's double points, so we're still in with a chance if we win some more races! Come on! Let's show them!"

Inspired by Simon's courage, the team prepared for the next competition, which was a sort of novelty race to entertain the audience. This year, the race involved a sleeping bag, wheelbarrow, fishing wand, some furry worm-like toys in a barrel and a washing line on which the worms had to be hung. There were endless opportunities for things to go wrong, and they often did – not least because their ponies didn't particularly trust the long sticks with wriggly things dangling from the end – but perhaps they sensed their riders' determination to win, because the Bellsham Vale wheelbarrow was pushed over the finish line way ahead of all the others.

The flag race was something Joe and all the team had practised again and again, so that handling the flags and placing them with pinpoint precision had become second nature. After bending, it was Joe's favourite, but he knew he couldn't drop his concentration for a second.

Joe usually tried not to look at the other teams while the race was on, in case it distracted him, but he couldn't help noticing that they were lying in second place as he took Caroline's flag from her and set off. Lightning seemed to know how important this was. All their training came together in those precious seconds as they galloped to the far end, put the flag in place as they turned, sped to the midway container, removed a flag and raced to the line to hand it over to Simon. They were now in the lead!

Simon was the last to go, and he was being chased by Harry for the Angus team. Fortune's changes of pace were quicker and more fluent than Rolo's, and she gradually forged ahead, winning by a length. The scores went up. The Oakley team was first; two points ahead of the Angus and three ahead of the Bellsham Vale. There was still a chance, if they did well in the sack race and the others didn't. There was still a chance!

The big sack race was the final competition because it required a tremendous team effort.

Lucy had twisted her ankle slightly in the stepping stones race, so they decided she should hold the ponies for this one. Joe and Simon were the fastest runners, so they ran beside Caroline on Minstrel and Sarah on Flicka as they charged down to Lucy at the far end. There, the riders dismounted, Lucy held the ponies and Caroline, Sarah, Joe and Simon raced back to a large sack in the centre of the arena. Joe was fit, but he was gasping for breath when they all climbed into the sack and took hold of the corners, as they'd rehearsed over and over again. The main thing now was to keep in time. If anyone missed a beat they'd all fall over . . . Jump, jump, jump . . . They jumped in unison and the audience roared encouragement . . . Jump, jump . . . Every muscle in Joe's body screamed with exhaustion . . . Jump, jump . . . The Oakley team next to them was down! Don't think about it – *focus* – jump, jump . . . Nearly there! Push to the limit . . .

Jump, jump, jump . . . They jumped over the finish line and collapsed, exhausted. Had they won?

The results were displayed: Angus, Bellsham Vale, Devon and Somerset and Oakley.

That meant the Angus team had won the Prince Philip Cup, with the Bellsham Vale a close second. Joe saw Harry and his team mates jumping up and down, hugging each other and laughing with delight. Couldn't have happened to a nicer guy, he thought, feeling almost as pleased as if it had been him. Joe and his team mates hugged each other in a rather more subdued way, and then he went over to congratulate Harry.

Soon it was the prize-giving. The commentator announced that the Angus team had won the Prince Philip Cup and the Devon and Somerset had won the stable management cup.

"There's always next year," Joe said quietly to Caroline. "I'll give Mum a leaf blower for Christmas!"

Joe and his team mates set off around the ring behind the Angus team, while the audience clapped in time to the music. The spotlights picked out Harry and a girl called Camilla as they held the cup up between them.

Lightning arched her neck, pricked her ears and cantered along joyfully, as if to say, "Let's party! We've had a great time, and that's what matters."

*

The evening wasn't over yet. All six teams had to take part in the Grand Finale.

"One last effort, then you can have a holiday," Joe whispered to Lightning as they stood waiting to be called in. She flicked back a neat golden ear to listen, then both ears went forwards as the curtain parted. They cantered into the arena team by team, splitting into two arcs before lining up as a guard of honour for the other prize-winning horses and ponies entering the arena.

Harry was directly in front of Joe, on the opposite side of the arena. They grinned at each other. Joe thought Fortune looked as beautiful as any of the champions filing past them. He could hardly take in the fact she'd be coming back with them to Newbridge Farm.

Yes, it's been quite a day, Joe thought. Emily's going to have Lightning and I'm going to have Fortune; two of the best games ponies in the country; two of the luckiest people in the world. He wondered how Fortune got her name. Perhaps, like Lightning, it was inspired by her parents' names. Perhaps she'd cost a fortune – or could it be something to do with fortune-telling and luck? He thought of Nellie, sitting up there in the audience with his family and friends, and what she'd said about fortune-telling on Christmas Day. And that made him think about his horseshoe lucky charm and the wishing shoe under his bed. A smile slowly spread across Joe's face. Oh my goodness, he thought. Of course! She's one of my remaining horseshoe wishes: Fortune!

That only leaves one more to go . . .

Don't miss

Joe and the Race to Rescue,

the third book in the trilogy,
coming soon.

Author's Notes

First, I must apologise to the Pony Club and the organisers of the Prince Philip Cup for re-writing the history books. The Bellsham Vale Pony Club is a figment of my imagination, but the other Pony Club branches mentioned in this story are real and they have all competed in the Prince Philip Cup recently.

The Devon and Somerset Pony Club is our local branch here on Exmoor. When our children were younger they both took part in mounted games, although not to senior level, and they were coached by Marcus and Bella Capel. The Capels have been involved with the Prince Philip Cup for many years, as both trainers and organisers. In 2010 their son Rory was in the victorious Devon and Somerset team, with Bella as their coach. Lightning in this book was inspired by Rory's pony Danny.

I'm very grateful to the Capel family for helping me with this story from start to finish. Rory and a fellow team member, Scarlett Cooksley, spent a whole morning showing me how different races are ridden and giving me step-by-step demonstrations of how they vault on and jump off their ponies. They also talked me through a recording of the Devon and Somerset team riding to victory, giving me a wonderful insight into how it feels.

Bella and Marcus contributed lots of ideas and information, as well as giving up their valuable time at the Horse of the Year Show to take me 'backstage' to the stables and lorry park, where I had the opportunity to talk to some of the participants. As if that wasn't enough, Marcus and Rory both read through the first draft for me and made useful comments. Many thanks.

David Walker, a friend who is a vet, was also a great help. I asked his advice when I was writing about

Treacle becoming ill with colic. Unfortunately, a few of our horses have had colic in the past, so I know how distressing it can be.

I've also experienced the pain of losing a much-loved pony or horse unexpectedly. Sadly, it's something most owners have to face sooner or later, which is why I felt it was justified to include such a traumatic event in this story.

Mark Rashid is an American horse trainer who has written some excellent books about his experiences helping all sorts of horses and horse owners. He also teaches aikido, and applies many of the principles of aikido to horsemanship. His ideas on the subject really struck a chord with me when I read them, and I have found them useful when handling our own horses, especially our free-living Exmoor ponies. Andrew Medland, instructor at aikido shudokan, kindly allowed me to observe some of his lessons and lent me several books about aikido, for which I am very grateful.

There is a strong theme of farriery throughout this trilogy. Our farrier, Clive Ley, and his assistants, Josh and Dusty, put up with me watching them at work, taking photos and asking endless questions about horseshoes and shoeing. Their input was really useful, and chocolate biscuits are now assured when they come to our farm to shoe our horses!

I'm also very grateful to Nic Barker, our local "barefoot farrier", for sharing so much information with me about horse hoof rehabilitation and keeping horses unshod. She suggested a scenario for Lightning's recovery from apparently incurable lameness, based on her experiences with many similar cases.

After I'd written *Joe and the Hidden Horseshoe* I was interested to hear that the Capels used to have a talented games pony that became lame when shod but was fine when ridden barefoot.

Ideas for little things to include in my stories have come from many different sources. For instance, my Uncle David keeps his hens in a luxurious chicken house, complete with automatic drawbridge, which he calls Cluckingham Palace.

When our children were in the Pony Club, there was a pony called Mindy who belonged first to Gemma Edwards and then her brother, Darren. Mindy and the Capels' pony, Dorlyn, were so responsive that they could do mounted games without a bridle or head collar. Both Gemma and Darren rode at HOYS, and Darren is now a successful jockey and columnist for the *Horse and Hound*.

Jane Westcott and Penny Crane, two friends with children who've ridden in top-level Pony Club mounted games teams, also gave me ideas. For Jane an area competition in a particularly cold, wet field was an abiding memory, and for Penny there was the parents' competitiveness over the stable management competition at HOYS – leaf blowers were mentioned!

Many thanks to Fiona Kennedy and Felicity Johnston, my editors at Orion Children's Books, for giving me a perfect combination of freedom, guidance and encouragement.

And, of course, I would like to thank my husband, Chris, for his support, his illustrations and for the horses he's shared with me over the years.

Victoria Eveleigh
North Devon
January 2013

If you have enjoyed Joe's story,
you'll also love

A Stallion Called Midnight.

Here is a preview of the first chapter.

1

Jenny fled up the stony track from the village. "I won't go! *I won't!*" she shouted.

The wind snatched her words and carried them over the sea towards the mainland – towards that other world which had played little part in her life, until now.

"I'm perfectly happy living with Dad," she said to herself, "and I've got plenty of friends. There are the islanders, lighthouse-keepers, fishermen, summer workers, visitors; you can't have many more friends than that! So why does Dad think I need to make friends and learn about the world? Why will it be *good* for me to go away to that stupid school?"

"*Stupid, stupid school*" Jenny screamed into the wind.

She struggled to shut the gate at Quarter Wall. Then she turned and ran, with the wind chasing her, towards the quarries.

What if nobody likes me? she worried. What if I don't like them? It'll be like going to prison. Miles from Lundy, miles from Dad and, worst of all, miles from Midnight.

Jenny couldn't remember life without Midnight. He'd been the herd stallion since before she was born. He was the king, and Lundy was his kingdom. He roamed where he liked, jumping the walls with ease, and he took orders from nobody. Everyone who had tried to catch and tame him had failed miserably. Everyone except Jenny – but that was their secret.

Jenny picked her way down the slippery path to the old quarries, knowing where she'd choose to shelter from a south-westerly gale if she were a pony.

She was right. The ponies were in the second quarry, protected from the elements by the massive walls which made a kind of open cave looking out to sea. It was a peaceful sanctuary, while the storm raged all around and waves crashed against the rocks below.

Three foals had been born so far. Jenny sat down on

a slab of granite, and watched as they played together. She loved their ruffled, fluffy coats. Two foals were a creamy colour with pale grey legs. They'd probably end up golden dun with black points, like Midnight. The third was a light roan. Foals had to be the best baby animals in the world.

The mares dozed or wandered around picking at the plants that grew between the stones. They took no notice of the small, slender girl in their midst.

Jenny had spent so much time with the ponies that they probably thought she was another feral animal – once domesticated but now wild, like them. She liked the idea. Mrs Hamilton was always calling her a wild child.

"Why, oh *why?*" Jenny cried out, startling a couple of mares nearby. "Oops, sorry!" she said, lowering her voice. "I mean, why does anything have to change? Why can't Mrs Hamilton carry on teaching me? She must have done a pretty good job so far, or I wouldn't have got that scholarship, would I? And why was I told that exam was just a test to see how well I was doing?"

She gazed at the idyllic scene before her, and sighed. "I can't go away! I *can't!*" she said.

As if in agreement, Midnight walked up and nuzzled her short brown hair.

Jenny looked into his extraordinary midnight-blue eyes. "I wish I was a pony, Midnight. Life's simple for you, isn't it? You don't have to worry about exams and schools, or being sent to the mainland. All you have to do is find water, food and shelter."

Midnight gave a snort.

Jenny's cold fingers snuggled into the warm, soft hair under his thick mane. "Okay, so you have to take care of the mares and foals, I suppose, but that's not a hard job, is it? They pretty well take care of themselves, leaving you plenty of time to do as you please." She stood up on the granite slab and leaned over Midnight's broad back.

He shifted his weight slightly, but didn't move away.

Without a second thought, Jenny leapt lightly onto him, and sat there as if it were the most natural thing in the world. It didn't even occur to her that riding a wild stallion without a saddle or bridle was dangerous.

He wandered along the old quarry terrace, nibbling at the sparse vegetation. Jenny just sat there and talked about anything and everything.

Midnight and Jenny seemed to have an understanding; he allowed her to sit on his back, and she let him do as he pleased – mainly because she didn't know how to get him to do anything else.

"I wish I could ride properly," Jenny told him. "Then we could gallop over the island, jumping everything in our way. Wouldn't that be fun?"

Riding lessons were the one thing Jenny longed

for which she couldn't get on Lundy. Nobody else on the island seemed particularly interested in the ponies, beyond the fact they were nice to look at and had become a traditional part of Lundy – almost as popular as puffins with the tourists.

If only Mum . . . Jenny began to think, and then stopped herself. Dad said "if onlys" could drive you mad, and he was right.

By the time they got back to the quarry, Jenny's jeans were cold and clammy from Midnight's damp coat. They clung uncomfortably, chilling her body to shivering point.

"Time to go home and face the music," she said, giving Midnight a farewell rub on his shoulder. His lips quivered in ecstasy, and his eyes started to close.

"You big baby!" she teased. "It's lucky nobody else knows what a softy you are. Promise me you'll stay wild with everyone else, won't you? You'll stay safe and free as long as you're wild."

Midnight nudged Jenny with his nose. "Good boy," she said, scratching him under his chin. "Now, I really must be going."

Although Jenny was cold she ambled home reluctantly, taking the longer route through the north entrance to the quarries. The wind had calmed to a fresh breeze and a watery sun, like a torch with flat batteries, hung low in the sky. She hadn't realised how late it was.

As she walked past the farm buildings she saw her dad, Robert Medway, walking towards her with his long, easy stride. There was no escape; she'd have to talk to him.

"Thank goodness you're back. I was beginning to worry," he said. "I've just fed your animals for you. Do you want to help me with the chickens?"

She scuffed some gravel with her foot. "Okay."

"I'll get the corn, and you can collect the eggs," he said.

Jenny never tired of egg-collecting; it was like hunting for treasure. She went to the back of the wooden chicken shed, and opened the flap covering the nesting boxes.

The rusty hinges creaked.

She felt inside, her fingers searching for smooth eggs nestling in the straw. Instead, they dipped into the slimy contents of a jagged eggshell. As she withdrew her fingers something furry writhed against them. She snatched her hand away and peered cautiously into the long, dark box.

A large rat glared back, whiskers twitching, surrounded by a gooey mess of broken eggshells. It leapt out of the box and ran for cover under the shed.

Jenny screamed and jumped back, dropping the flap with a bang.

Dad hurried over, corn spilling from the feed scoop in his hand. "What's happened? Are you all right?"

"A rat! A really big one! Under there!" she squeaked. "All the eggs are broken! Ruined!"

Dad swore. "They've been in the vegetable garden too; it's a never-ending battle. Poor old you!" He hugged his daughter, holding her close.

Jenny loved his hugs. They were safe and solid.

"Ah well, rabbit stew for supper tonight," Dad said.

All the tensions of the day welled up and exploded inside Jenny, like a wave crashing against rocks. She burst into tears.

"Hey, what's up?"

"Everything! I hate rats and I hate rabbit stew!" she wailed into her father's coat.

He stroked her damp hair. "I bet they don't eat rabbit stew at St Anne's."

Oh no! Jenny thought. Here comes the lecture.

Dad hugged her tightly, engulfing her thin body in his strong arms. "I'm so proud of you," he said. "A scholarship to St Anne's really is a great achievement, you know."

"But I don't want to go, Dad! I know I'll hate it there!" She glanced up at him. "And why didn't you tell me it was a scholarship exam? Why did you lie?"

"Oh, Jenny! I thought you'd love to go away to school and be with girls your own age for a change, rather than being stuck here the whole time. I couldn't afford to send you without the money for the scholarship, but I didn't want you to feel under pressure or to be disappointed if you failed. It was a white lie, I suppose."

"What's a white lie?"

"A lie told to avoid hurting someone's feelings."

"Oh. Well, it didn't work, did it?" Jenny looked up again, and met her father's concerned gaze. "This is my home. I love it here. Why does anything have to change? Please don't make me go!"

"Of course I won't *make* you go, Jenny, but you'll be missing the greatest opportunity of your life – and a lot of fun, too." Dad lowered his voice to a secret whisper. "I've heard there are stables nearby, and riding's an optional extra. You'd be able to have lessons every week. Would you like that?"

Riding lessons! Jenny thought. Perhaps if she went away to school for a little while – just a term or two – she could learn to ride and then come home again for good. Riding lessons cost a lot of money, though. And she'd need riding clothes, like the girls in the *Princess Pony Annual* Mrs Hamilton had given her for Christmas. It would all be hopelessly expensive.

"Would you like riding lessons?" Dad asked again.

"Of course I would, but we can't afford it," she

answered. "Also, I'll need boots, a hat, jodhpurs, a jacket and a yellow polo neck." She'd always longed for a yellow polo neck. She imagined herself looking like the girl on the front cover of the annual.

"I expect we'll manage somehow. Summer's coming up, so you'll be able to earn some money in the Hotel, and I'll get all the extra jobs I can. If you want riding lessons, you shall have them."

Jenny couldn't help smiling now. "Do you mean it?"

Dad smiled back. "Of course I mean it."

"I suppose school *could* be okay, if there's riding as well."

"I bet it'll be more than okay. It'll be great fun, you wait and see." Dad put his arm round Jenny's shoulder and turned towards home. "Meg! That'll do!" he called to his sheepdog as she tried, in vain, to get at the rat under the chicken shed.

A new world of possibilities opened up to Jenny. "Perhaps I could keep my own pony at the stables," she said, secretly thinking of Midnight.

Dad laughed and ruffled her hair. "Don't push your luck, young lady!"

Ah well, it was worth a try.